The Cockslayer

The Cockslayer
Rick Mc Callister

CASASOLA LLC, 1619 1St St NW, Apt C Washington, DC 20001 *
Apartado 2171, Tegucigalpa, Honduras *

info@casasolaeditores.com

The Cockslayer ®
Title in spanish: *El matagallos*®

ISBN-10: 1942369018
ISBN-13: 978-1-942369-01-1

First Edition printed in the United State of America.

Designed by Casasola Editores © 2015

***

TABLE OF CONTENTS

Dedicated to the people of Cuscatancingo.

***

I beg FORGIVENESS and FORGETTING
from all those I have satirized.

***

Thanks to Abigaíl Guerrero
for her critical eye and her suggestions.

Lupus est homo homini, non homo,
quom qualis sit non novit.

***

Man is a wolf among men, not a man,
when he fails to know his neighbor.

Titus Marcius Plautus

Translator's Preface

I wrote this puppy in Spanish and also translated it into English. Given that no translation can ever match the original, my apologies. There are terms and names that come from Salvadoran Spanish, *inter alii*. Some are meant to be somewhat opaque, in order to preserve the tone of the novel, e.g. a few passages in foreign languages. But the diligent reader will figure this out. Others are purely regional, such as *Tecolote*, the last name of the protagonist. *Tecolote* literally means "barn owl, lesser owl, etc." in Central America and Mexico. In slang, it can mean "nerd, dork, four eyes, gay." Word play, intertextuality and satire are important parts of this novel, especially among languages and authors, but the novel can be read at various levels. The novice reader will enjoy it just as much. For those who know Spanish well, I recommend the original in Spanish. Read and enjoy. I have kept quoted material in the original language, followed by English translations. Note that in the original Spanish title "*Matagallos*", *gallo* refers to the cock as rooster, not as male organ, only in English does it have its dual meaning, which serendipitously works even better.

Introitus

Rorate, caeli, desuper, et nubes pluant iustum:
aperiatur terra, et germinet Salvatorem.[*]

Congratulations! You just got hold of a copy of
The Cockslayer! I didn't say "buy" but rather
"get hold of" because if someone bought it for
you as a gift or if you read it free at La Ceiba
Bookstore at Las Cascadas Hypermall sitting in
the seat in front of the show window, so much
the better. I'd be very happy to know you saved
money so you could spend it on your kids. Anyway, I hope they haven't charged you more than
five bucks. La Ceiba, La Casita, Prolibros and
all the other bookstores aren't ripoffs.

Maybe you have this book in your hand because it piqued your curiosity. After all, what
could a Gringo know about El Salvador? Why
would a Gringo write in Spanish when everybody
wants to learn English? How dare that Gringo
speak this way about the national institutions of
El Salvador if the United States is really fucked
these days. Well, you gotta read the book to find
all this out. But I'm gonna promise you I ain't
no sissified high-class punk-ass bitch from Mi-
ramonte, the kind that go around shitting all
over everything. They even curse the tit that fed
them. No way, dude. I wasn't in Escalón. I spent

---

* Cover us, clouds, from the heavens above, and let the clouds
rain down Justice: Let the earth open, and give fruit to a Savior.
[Isaiah 45:8]

my days in Cuzcatancingo, where a roll from *El Rosario* is a real treat, where *La Heladería 2 x 1* Ice Cream Parlor is a true delight, where those high class sissies who call themselves writers would shit their pants in fear.

So, bud, now you got this book in your hand. Go to the most comfortable corner of your pad, better yet, the patio, under the shade. Keep two or three *Pilseners* at arms length cause once you get started, you sure as shit ain't gonna wanna get up. Pass some bills to your old man or old lady so they can take the brats to the Parque Infantil so they don't disturb you. Even better, tell'em to bring you one of them dollar pizzas from *Panadería El Rosario*, cause if you have to get up in the middle of a chapter, you're gonna be bitching some serious shit.

And relax, dude, let the words flow, absorb them, dive into the plot. Think about how many Cockslayers you've known, how you dealt with them, how the bosses always gave'em raises and promotions, even though they never sweated a drop of work. Don't get pissed, cause the laughter this book produces is your revenge. This book is written against every asshole who rose through the ranks without working and against every boss who pitted his employees against one another to take advantage of them. And since there are Cockslayers in every country in the world, that's how I could write about one in El Salvador.

And don't you worry. This book is completely fictitious and has nothing to do with you or your squeeze, or your job or with anyone you know. It doesn't even have anything to do with your boss, even if he is a son of 30,000 whores. It's just pure unadulterated bullshit. Life is too short for paranoia. You gotta enjoy life reading a awesome novel like this. Like the Romans said: *Accipe hoc*, that is--"suck it up."

Who is the Cockslayer?

Who are you, . . . who, who?
I really wanna know, . . . who who?

The Who

A man with a diseased mind and a soul so black
that he would obscure even the darkness of hell!
Reed Smoot, US Senator, 1930

Neto Tecolote always dreamed about being so much more than what he really was. He was never content with just being a pencil pusher in the worst administered department, in the most disorderly section, of the most corrupt, fraudulent and criminal organization, for the misfortune of society, under the aegis of the most insignificant ministry of the smallest country in Latin America. Yet he never ceased shouting to the four winds his sacred duty and patriotic fervor in serving children from families of limited means. "These poor abandoned creatures must be able to better themselves," he repeated with tears in his eyes, to his underlings, while hidden up his sleeve were the true reports of cash flows and expenditures, in the millions, that a well-known frozen country had so generously donated, to better the future of those poor abandoned little creatures that Neto so loudly whined about. He had to act the saint to cover up his true mediocre nature: while he was extorting bucks, sex and even chickens from those whom he had sworn to serve, it came to him naturally. Neto wasn't alone. His trusted employees, a team composed of sharks, deadbeats and suck-ups, supported him unconditionally.

In one of the most unexplained mysteries of this world, his specialized team never worked. They brazenly loafed around under his protection, mistreated the most humble teachers in the public schools, and took advantage of the organization's resources for their own use. They always claimed better results than the other team, which Neto described as a "shitload of doofuses" composed of personnel blessed with an authentic spirit of service who had mastered their profession. Neto had a clinical eye. His training as a psychologist helped him select those who formed his specialized team. All that work was necessary to triumph, because he was aware of his futile nature. He knew he was nothing more than a completely useless wanker, a man so gray that he seemed transparent and, therefore, harmless to the players in that corruption machine that siphoned off money that arrived from abroad in the form of loans intended to alleviate the misery caused by centuries of bad government and proximity to the United States of America. His impotence drove him nuts, to the point of turning him into a demon with the face of a doofus.

He was always eager to rise above his name. How much he would have loved to have been a Wolf, an Eagle, a Lion, anything more worthy of respect than a Tecolote, or barn owl. "Ay, why such an ugly bird!" he muttered to himself.

-Why such a scary, repugnant bird that lives in holes, that only flies in the shadows, that doesn't kill anything other than scared little chicks before they can become cocks or hens. Cocks? Yuck! I've never known a more disgusting animal than a cock! Yuck!

And while a marked sign of disgust was written on his face, he thought that a really awesome name like that of the rocker Antonio "Viper" Morán, or the scientist Carlos "Kanga" Nájera would have saved his self-esteem. But life cursed him with a name steeped in bad luck:

When the *tecolote** sings,
the indian dies,
it may not be true,
but it happens.

The *tecolote* sings
and the indian dies,
when they lift up the basket
this happens.

In truth, wherever Neto Tecolote went, he sowed destruction, at first more so due to his unfitness as a man than for his machinations. Only later would he live for the pleasure of destroying his fellow man.

He didn't even like his first name, Néstor, named for "the master of the courtly word, the orator of clear voice," the mentor of the Greeks in Troy. It meant "returner, he who returns to his origins." Some folks, however, made the mistake of supposing that Neto was a nickname for Ernesto. And Neto corrected that lickety-split.

-¡Me llamo Néstor, no soy Ernesto!

* Tecolote: Barn owl

Because, if you have to be nicknamed Neto, it's much better to be a Néstor than an Ernesto, a name popularized in a dramatic work by Oscar Wilde.

But while almost all the Ernestos of the world, from the Argentine Che to the Ernestos of the Ejército Revolucionario del Pueblo, could rise above their name, Neto drowned in his own impotence. The pure, honest truth is that he was a pathetic bastard, starting with his name. He only wanted to have what others had and if he couldn't get it, he was hellbent on destroying their happiness.

Even more curious than his first name, was his surname, *Tecolote*, originally *Tekúlut* in Nawat, the name of a bird of prey, from Nawat tet "stone" and *kúlut* "scorpion, penis" or "stone cock," or te- "person (object) and *kúlut*; i.e. "cockster", but more likely an apocope of *teku* "lord" and *kulut* "penis" –hence "cock master".

Now that we know who the Tecolote is, let's delve into how he arrived at such a vile and pathetic state.

Book I:
Neto's Formative Years

Outta my way, you small-town clowns
This country boy is comin' to town.

Bill Kirchen

Now you have an idea of who the Cockslayer is. You've run into a shitload of assholes just like him –dickweeds who've manage to somehow become ballbusters with only half a nut. Here in this book, you'll see how he was born and how he came to be –let's say, his *tonal* and his *nawal.* For the native Meso-Americans, one's *tonal,* or birthday, offered important insight into one's nature, or rather innate tendencies. The *nawal* was one's spirit companion and indicated one's character, the path one would choose and one's relationship with the rest of the community. These factors are strong, but not determinative in any way, since any brave soul with good character can overcome them or only use them for good.

You'll see how Neto was treated in his youth, and how he treated those closest to him, and how this influenced the rest of his life. We'll see how some saw him for what he was early on in life and what they did to root out that evil flower before it gave fruit. We'll see how some grow poison ivy as if it were a rose in order to infect this beautiful world we live in with its venom.

This section is a bit longer than the "Introitus", so you're gonna have to rest a couple of hours beforehand and have a beer or two and some munchies close at hand, just in case you wanna keep on reading. Don't commence drinking too early, since there's nothing worse than to have to get up and take a piss while you're laughing your ass off.

Birth of the Tecolote

Eso explica en parte mi problema.˙
[Roque Dalton. *"No, no siempre fui tan feo"*]

Neto Tecolote was a man as ill born and in ill standing in every sense, a man outside of the human conventions to which he so desperately aspired, but which were so brutally derailed by his actions and alienation from the company of mankind. He never felt emotions or sentiments like most people. He was born a ball of flesh with a rigid and inexpressive face that marked him for the rest of his life. During his first months of life, his own mother felt terror when she approached him. Strangely, his body gave off no odor, and apart from the tears he spilled only when he was hungry or thirsty, he never showed any kind of feelings. She understood that the soul of this ill born creature was sealed shut. She wanted to rid herself of him, but she had the misfortune of consulting Doctor Heraclio Barba, a retired forensic doctor, avid reader of novels centering on serial killers, who in return for three colones treated the poor in his own house. Dr. Heraclio told her that a newborn without any odor would doubtlessly become a murderous psychopath. But that given his strange experiences as a reader and forensic doctor, he recommended a cleansing with witchdoctors. And she did so. Neto was sub-

---

* This, in part, explains my problem.

jected to strong spiritualist sessions all the time he was being nursed, in which they made him ingest a strong malodorous brew made of ingredients known only to the witchdoctor, I mean doctor, prepared over flames in the heart of the little that remained of the forest. While the child ingested the infusion, the doctor consulted *Brujerías típicas de Cuzcatlán* and intoned:

Makisa ne nawal
Makikcha librar ni mal
Ken nik tajtánik
*Tutéku Tekúnal**

Finally, *ignotum per ignotius*, he managed to produce his own odor, as impure, nauseating and fetid as a rotten egg. But the rigidity of his expression never changed. It so happened that his spirit companion appeared that night, a barn owl sitting in a tree above the fire, devouring a chick. The tecolote, bird of ill omen, servant of Satan, only accompanied the vilest critters. From the remote times of the *Popol Vuh*, tecolotes have been faithful to the Lords of Xibalbá, the Mayan Hell.

Neto was a psychopath from birth, just as Dr. Heraclio Barba revealed, destined as much by his *nawal* as by his *tonal* –given that he was born Friday, November 13, when Pluto was in the House of Scorpion. His stiff tortilla face nev-

---

* May the spirit companion come forth
  May he free us from evil
  as we pray
  to Our Lord of the Burning Coals.

er reflected any type of emotion. He was as ugly and evil as Satan. A Tecolote he was born, and as a Tecolote he would live, and after death, he would become a tecolote with wings and feathers. *Aut Tecolote aut nihil!*

The only child of Ms Xúchit Tekúlut and her employer, Lord Austin Tavernor Owlsleigh, *Attaché Militaire* of the Government of *His Britannic Majesty*, George VI, future benefactor of the prestigious Academia Inglesa de Cuzcatlán, then a rogue, womanizer and drunkard, son of Lady Constance Olivia Mellors de Owsleigh, the wife of the notorious sodomite, the previous Lord Owsleigh, and her chauffeur, a certain Mister James Clifford Chatterley. The poor thing washed and ironed for the aforementioned Lord Owlsleigh, until one day, under the influence of a bottle of Tic Tack, he returned her favor by giving her a good ironing of his own. When his wife noticed her belly, she threw her out in the street, not before citing every chapter and verse of the eminently distinguished *Salvadoran Dictionary of Cursewords and Gratuitous Insults of the Royal Cuzcatlan Academy of the Language.*

Without any destination and homeless, Ms Tekúlut walked under the rain for two days until she reached the Barranca del Cusuco, on the outskirts of Apopa, the only place she could ever consider as home. There, many years before, Ms Ixchel, Xúchit's mother, took refuge from the bloody massacre of '32. The poor woman fled Izalco after being brutally raped by a company of soldiers under the command of General Maximiliano Hernández Martínez. After her cruel deflowering, Ixchel ran naked until she fell into the ravine.

After returning to where she left her umbillicus, Ms Xúchit built a *champa*, a hut upon a huge rock above the creek, near her mother's tomb. There, she had a vision of a tecolote seated upon a nopal cactus, devouring a chick. That image accompanied her many solitary nights. She didn't know if she would survive. Sometimes, she plucked a little fish from the creek to assuage the hunger that tormented her. A friend lent her some change, so she could buy *alhuashte* and black corn. It was thanks to that act of kindness that she began to earn a meager living selling *atol shuco*. That's how she took care of her son, even though it gave Neto an intense feeling of shame that haunted him the rest of his life. To be the bastard child of a *shuquera* was an abomination. He couldn't handle it. For him, being a *shuquera* was proof of absolute destitution. Only a completely worn out, abandoned, illiterate, penniless woman, without skills or family would spend the whole day filling and washing gourds of *atol shuco* in front of the bus stop.

He always recalled that at school, he did everything he could to trick her so she wouldn't show up for Mother's Day celebrations. He was ashamed of her. His mother noticed it, but she never reproached him. She was so devoted and kind that she pardoned everything, even when he ate all the chicken, that is, when there was an opportunity to buy some. He never recognized his mother's devotion, that she lived only for him, and that she had no luxuries or vices.

That was the only way they could survive.

Survive, but not live, since atol shuco represented the country's genuine Native American culture. It was completely unknown among decent folk, who were used to eating grilled meat or steaks. And, in his heart, Neto truly believed himself to be a knight born in the wrong time and place.

Even the ingredients of atol shuco are one hundred per cent Native American: 1 pound of black corn, red beans, cock's tail chile, y alhuashte (ground pumpkin seed), all boiled together in a gloppy mass. To anyone who boasted of Spanish blood, the preparation seemed more like a witch's brew: let the corn ferment for a day, strain it, add salt, cook it until the sour semi-putrified stench is gone, mix it with par-boiled beans, alhuashte and cock's tail chile. It's served in a gourd. To top it off, the name of the brew itself, atol shuco (atul xuku) means "shitty water" in Nawat.

It was during his first years when Neto began his tecolotic attacks. Ms Xúchit noticed that whenever she managed to get some chicken, Neto's eyes bulged with happiness, his arms began to flap till they were ready and he began to chant a tune similar to a rap. This was a startling sound to any Native American used to the clean sounds of nature. Sometimes, she thought it would be better not to bring him chicken, but she couldn't deprive him of the food that she managed to get for her offspring with so much hard labor. Full of fear, she kneeled to pray everytime Neto sang:

Dame da-me da-me todo el pollo.
Dame el poder. Dame el poder
Lo quiero. Lo quiero
*Dame Dame todo el pollo. *

His demand for chicken was ever greater and since Ms Xúchit couldn't fulfill it, Neto began to steal chickens in the neighborhood. His mother gave him a good ass-whipping to stop his bad habit and made him return even the feathers of the chickens he stole. Since he saw the woman's firm determination, he had no recourse but obey, but some tendencies are persistent in the nature of psychopaths and it was then when Neto discovered the immense pleasure that chicken blood provoked in him. He stretched out in pleasure when he heard the desperate cackling of hens, the flapping of cock's wings who futilely tried to defend themselves as Neto nailed his fingernails and teeth into them. He didn't need a knife. When everyone began guarding their chicken coops, he settled for opening up an orifice in them, so he could easily suck their blood. If, by chance, there were no birds, he would attack pigs or other animals with an icepick, but he wouldn't consume them. It was just to seek revenge against those who deprived him of his tecolotic pleasure. Those were the first manifestiations of the mythological Chupacabras in El Salvador.

* Gimme, gimme, gimme all the chicken
  Gimme the power. Gimme the power.
  I want it. I want it.
  Gimme, gimme all the chicken.

Neto learned how to devour a whole bird without suffering stomach problems. His victims, uncountable cocks and hens, would have preferred traditional techniques for beheading birds. If only those poor birds could speak. Hundreds suffered a slow and brutal death in the jaws of Neto Tecolote, who pulsated with pleasure with every bite.

Years later, when he enjoyed the position granted to him by the forces of evil, he didn't feel the least remorse for how he treated his mother. Then, he realized that if she hadn't have been a woman of solid principles, he would have sent her out to prostitute herself, just to keep chicken on the table for every meal. And then he would have been the pimp of his own mother. He never knew why, but when the stress of the job tormented him, he gave himself up to the following fantasy:

- Old woman, hurry up, now. Go to your corner.

-Son, I can't take this life, just let me sell shuco.

-You're nothing but my bitch. How can you think of selling *shuco*, that disgusting shit. Go to your johns. Hurry up and wiggle your ass good this time, don't be a lazy shit. If you don't bring me chicken tonight, I won't let you in the house.

Almost everyday, he gave free rein to his perverse mind. And in the sublime moment of his disgusting fantasies, sketching out a smile, he'd exclaim:

-Neto Tecolote, the bird psychopath

-Neto, the heartless pimp of hi

First Flights of the Tecolote

¿Y
si llega
la
oportunidad?

Roque Dalton

Given that he inherited his color and his nose from his English father, his mother decided to Hispanicize their last name to hide their Native American roots. His name, Néstor Homero Tecolote, provoked no end of laughter during his youth. Scrawny and light-skinned, half blind, he had to squint in order to see, until one day, his mother won a hundred colones in the lottery to buy him glasses. Tall and skinny, with long hair and thick glasses, he looked more tecolote than human, especially when he sat hunchback, with his nose buried in a book. His inexpressive face was as rigid as a two-by-four, emotionless and unfeeling, a psychopath in the making, although it would take various years to become obvious to everyone. He was as ugly and evil as Satan. And since he was neither fish nor fowl, the other kids laughed at him till their bellies split. Everyday they threw rocks at him and shouted:

Tecolote, zopilote
hijo de cerote.
Neto Homero, Teculero,
te van a romper el trasero.[*]

Neto Homero, as his mother called him, completely ignored them. Since he knew his father was a lord, he walked erect with his nose held high. He never broke words with anyone. He saw his time in Apopa as a testing ground to turn him into the true man that he would be as soon as he could get out of the Barranca del Cusuco.

One day, Ricardo Guatón Basovia, known as "Pelo Cagado", or "Shit Hair," due to the splotches of gray in his hair, who was the closest thing to a friend to Neto at eight years of age, told him about the king who wanted to learn how to fly. The king offered a thousand pieces of gold and the hand of his only daughter to anyone who could teach him how to fly. To those who failed, he cut off their heads. Every able-bodied young man went to the palace with ideas, but nothing worked. The country reeked from all the decapitated heads. Then, one day, a peasant arrived named Bartolo Naco, with a really cool plan. One day, while was herding his goats, he saw a fledgling tecolote on a limb. The branch broke, and the young tecolote flapped

---

[*] Barn owl, buzzard
son of a turd
Neto Homero, ass-fuck bird
They're gonna split your ass.

its wings until it soared to the clouds.

Neto, who stood there with his jaw agape, decided to put the plan into practice. He told Ricardo to bring a saw from his dad, who was a carpenter. Ricardo tried to dissuade him.

-But, Neto... Neto. I still haven't...

-Hurry up, already, before nightfall, get a move on, now!

Ricardo kept trying to tell him something, but Neto pushed him toward his house. Ricardo returned with the saw. Meanwhile, Neto got some cardboard, glue and feathers, which he used to make wings.

-Neto, are you sure you wanna do this?... You didn't let me finish the story...

-Let's go, dumbass, it's about to get dark.

Neto climbed a mango tree, the tallest tree in the ravine. He carefully crept out to the end of one of the highest limbs. When he stopped trembling, he shouted to Ricardo.

-Cut the branch, quick!... Daedalus! If you could do it, I can too!

His flight, however, turned out more like that of Icarus. He flapped his wings as fast as he could, but he fell like a stone. First, he hit don Estanislao Barcia's roof. He bounced off and hit a blackberry bush, and then fell into the creek, which, rather than a stream, was an open sewer through which passed all the pestilent sewage of Apopa. He returned to the mango tree, where Ricardo was waiting for him.

-But, what happened?... You told me the king flew!

-You didn't let me finish the story... The king tried to fly, but he fell and died when his head smashed into a rock. The peasant married the princess and everyone lived happily ever after.

-You are one evil motherfucker!

And thus ended the only true friendship Neto would ever have in all his life. But destiny would bring them together one day again. Heartless, astute, lying, evil hearted, ass licking, bad intentioned like no one else, don Ricardo Guatón Basovia was destined to become his right hand man many years later. The pain of the fall did not hurt nearly so much as the shame that marked him forever. News of his deed caught flight and when everyone found out, they threw chicken feathers, eggshells and spitballs at the "Cock-Hen" in school. More daring classmates ventured to sketch obscene drawings of disproportionate cocks of different types engaged in immoral acts. Every time he left school, the Cock Boys surrounded him, with their hands under their armpits making chicken sounds. And although he never confessed it, for the rest of his life, Neto could never enjoy a cockfight, or be in the presence of cocks without his stomach turning. What's more, he couldn't look at himself naked in the mirror, or have sex with girls, without remembering those disgusting immoral cocks that assaulted his memory, his manhood, his strength and his sexual appetite at every moment. From then on, the word "cock" was banned from his vocabulary. His internal life became a secret and atrocious battle against that repugnant and pestilent yardbird.

For some time before the terrible confrontation with the Cock Boys, he managed to dissipate his obsessive thoughts toward that type of fowl. With this in mind, he shut himself up in the library, where he read travel books and he made an effort to pronounce the foreign languages he would have to learn later as he traveled around the world. He dreamed of being an *hidalgo, "hijo de algo,"* a son of something, rather than the bastard son of no one that he was. In his fantasies, he was a playboy, a Ramfis Trujillo, a Porfirio Rubirosa, a James Bond 007, en spite of the fact that he was a zero, zero, zilch. Even so, he had visions of strolling through the Casino Royale with a beauty under each arm as the orchestra played *El cumbanchero*:

El cumban-cumban-cumban-chero chero chero
cumbanchero, cumbanchero que se va
el bongo-bongo-bongo-bongo-sero sero sero
bongosero, bongonsero que se va
el Teco-teco-teco-teco-lote lote lote
Tecolote, Casanova que se va.

The Cocks

El martes de carnaval
un gallo muerto de risa
salió en mangas de camisa
del Hospital General

Juan Martínez Villerga

Rara avis that he was, at school he became the constant object of teasing from the Cock Boys, a gang of kids his age who slicked back their hair with Brylcream, who greeted one another with a cock-a-doodle-doo deep in their throats and who bragged of never leaving untouched any "hen" in the neighborhood. On April Fool's Day, they strutted out to drink in the *cantina* to prove how *macho* they were.

To amuse their elders, they decided to dance the "Cock Dance." Don Celso, the barkeep, an old sailor, learned it in South America and taught it to everyone. He'd worked all his life to earn enough money to come home and build "La Minga," the only tavern in the neighborhood. Given that the name means "cueball," it obviously had a pool table, but it had little more to offer. The adventures of don Celso on the Seven Seas, however, were much more entertaining than anything on TV or the jukebox.

The customers pushed all the tables and chairs against the wall to form a space marked out in chalk. The Cock Boys prepared themselves. They all tucked in painted paper cock's tails into the backs of their pants and tied them up with a belt. Then they stretched out old red rubber gloves and placed them on their heads. They put in pieces of cardboard, so they'd stand up like an erect cock's comb. After that, they put on cowboy spurs. Then everyone grabbed a lit candle with his right hand. They formed a circle with everyone looking outwards. There they waited as the bartender carefully pulled an old scratched record from its jacket. He polished it with a soft, clean rag and placed Eva Ayllón's *Alcatraz* on the record player.

And so, the ruckus began. All the Cock Boys ran after one another, trying to set each other's paper tail on fire. They kicked out with their spurs toward anyone come up behind them and "winged" with their elbows, anyone next to them. Drops of blood fell all over the circle. The drunks began to point out their favorites and whipped out cash to bet on them. When Mamerto was the first to catch fire, they all erupted in applause and invited the "burnt ass" to have a cold one. One by one, the Cocks were eliminated ¬Jaime, Norberto, Jovel, Rigoberto y Manolo—until two were left. All the "burnt asses" awarded with beer and applause. Now, the supporters of each one of the survivors began to shove one another and insult each other's mother. Finally, Martín ducked and slid in behind, and set his opponent's tail on fire. They surely must have heard the screaming over in Honduras when they carried Martín around on their shoulders. Don Maximiliano Alvarado, the moneylender, happy with his earnings, treated him to a bottle of Tic-Tack, so he and his friends could drink like men.

When the afternoon was done, the Cock Boys were real fucked up. When they left the cantina, they could barely walk. Some of them began to puke their guts out. In front of the exit, they bumped into Neto. They went back inside, filled up some balloons with water and bombarded him till they turned him into Tecolote soup. They threw him down on the ground. Then they kicked his ass with their spurs. They wanted Neto to show how scared he was, but that was impossible. Not even in the gravest moments in his life, would he feel such an emotion. He was a born psychopath with a stiff tortilla face. He was as ugly and evil as Satan. Under these circumstances, they kept on torturing him. For desert, they shoved an empty bottle of Gallo beer up his ass, leaving him in the Hospital Bloom with a broken tailbone:

Tecolote, zopilote
hijo de cerote.
Neto Homero, Teculero,
*te rompieron el trasero.**

---

* Barn owl, bald buzzard
  son of a turd
  Neto Homero Assfuck
  they done broke your ass, my word.

Book II:
Rise to Power

Oh! Laugh you laughers
Oh! Laugh it up, you laughers
Laugh with laughter, laugh it up laughingly
Oh! Laugh laugh-it-up-ingly
Oh! Laughable laughdom –laughing it up by laughter
/ laugh lords
Laughingly, laughingly
Laugh it up, laughnessly, you laughterboys,
/ laughterboys
Little laughers, little laughers
Oh! Laugh you laughers
Oh! Laugh it up, you laughers!

Velimir Khlebnikov

I hope you're laughing without bounds, completely out of control, full throttle. Till your
squeeze, your brats and your neighbors can't
sleep from all the laughter coming out of your
mouth. Laughter is the best weapon invented
against assholes, so you have to take advantage of it without limits. And don't show pity for
any poor bastard. Cervantes wrote *Don Quix-
ote* so you would shit your britches laughing,
so you would join him in laughing at a drool-
ing tard with backward ideas. The priest who
wrote *Lazarillo de Tormes* is sitting on Cloud
Nine just waiting for you burst out laughing
at the misfortunes of that sorry sack of shit.
The only comfort that ultra-conservative, traitor
and proto-fascist Francisco Quevedo receives in
Hell is when you laugh at Pablos and the other
victims of his wrathful laughter.

I hope you're well prepared for your next

reading and that you're not just cramming junk food down your mouth while you're reading my words. Show some respect for both of us. Fix yourself a nice salad, some bean soup with chiles and lime, whatever you like it, some pickled veggies, some tamarind juice because good laughing requires the use of healthy muscles.

In this section, you'll see how Neto came to be boss, all the dirty rotten tricks he played, all the asses he sucked –not to mention licked. It's a little bit longer than the previous sections but I guaran-fucking-tee you're gonna piss the bed laughing.

Ahhhhh! All those songs you see scattered among the prose can be found on Google. Or better yet, almost all of them, cause I had to invent and translate a few from some God awful fucking languages such as Russian. And if you're lucky, you can find some on *YouTube*. You can also find the complete texts of the epigraphs on *Google*.

The Transfiguration of the Tecolote

*Y si alguien dice que esta historia
es esquemática y sectaria*

...

*que vaya a comer mierda
porque la historia y el poema
no son más que la puritita verdá.*

Roque Dalton

For various days, Neto lay unconscious in a deadly nightmare –a flock of cocks pecked at his eyes and other orifices, cock-a-doodle-dooing with spasms of joy, while the women of the neighborhood applauded, pointed at Neto, threw kisses and flashed their netherparts at the Cock Boys. From that moment on, he trembled every time he heard a yardbird. Everytime a chicken crossed his path, and everytime he heard an appliance commercial from *El Gallo Más Gallo* (The Cockiest Cock), he turned red with rage. Although this could only be noticed by someone really perceptive. It was hard to guess emotions in a rigid tortilla face such as Neto, a born psychopath. He was as ugly and evil as Satan.

He decided that his redemption lay in avenging himself against the avian race. He was born a Tecolote . . . and being a Tecolote would be his destiny. At that moment, a man arrived dressed in a jacket, tie, shirt, pants, hat, suspender, shoes and socks –all black with a strong odor of sulfur. He carried a black portfolio, from which he took out an enormous black book. He opened it up to page six hundred sixty six and pointed with his black pen to line six point six six.

-Sign here and everything you desire will be yours for your entire life; you will be the cause of much misfortune here in this *soi-disant* Republic of El Salvador, dedicated to my eternal enemy. You will be my greatest assistant here and for eternity.

Neto didn't waste a mini-second in handing over his soul to the Adversary. In the background, he heard an old blues tune:

I went down to the Crossroads
fell down on my knees
asked the Lord for mercy
"Save poor Neto if you please."

Neto began to have visions of the ceiba, the axis mundi, with leaves in heaven, its trunk on earth and its roots in the underworld. The world tree, the *póchotl, púchut, yaaxche, ceiba petandra, kapok, silk-cotton tree*, grew next to the crossroads. Underneath its shade sat a troop of pochtecas, merchants and spies for the Aztec Empire, seeking slaves for sacrifice. On the left was the *ciguanaba*, the *cegua*, the *llorona*, the *siwa nawal, witch woman* searching for her *cipitío*, her lost child, who played in the river with a pair of *cadejos*, devil dogs, one white, one black, with eyes of burning coals.

Ready for Liftoff

Houston, we have lift off

Ron Howard

After New Year's Day, Neto woke up with good news. Lord Owlsleigh had died of gout after a long and bibulous life. In his will, he left a scholarship for him to attend the Academia Inglesa de Cuzcatlán during his last year of high school. At that very moment, Neto realized that just as his sufferings brought joy to everyone else. In the same manner, others' suffering would be his delight.

At the Academy, Neto continued his solitary life. A man so removed from the knowledge of social customs was condemned to never find love or friendship. Whenever he saw a pretty or friendly girl, he would follow her from afar until she reached her house, but he never had the courage to speak to her. But the English notion of fair play and the erroneous idea that his behavior was due to his father's eccentricities gave him a critical space to develop his perverse nature. He received his diploma as a member of the founding class of that august institution. For that reason, the Academy took in any kind of student with open arms; that is, any who could pay full tuition. Given that he almost never spoke or bothered anyone, he would have graduated almost unperceived if not for his high school capstone thesis: *Líderes de genio e* *hierro*[*], a panegyric on the miracles of General Fidel Sánchez Hernández, President of the Republic, and the ever-ruling Partido de Conciliación Nacional.

His efforts were not in vain. Since almost all young people militated for change and desired a future in a democratic homeland with justice for all, Neto Tecolote took refuge in an imaginary past where everything belonged to him by divine right. One day, he received an invitation to attend a political forum where the future leaders of the fatherland could meet the country's rulers. His mother took out a loan from the moneylender, don Max Alvarado, to buy him his first suit, so he could make a good impression.

Upon entering the Teatro Nacional, Neto and his group received a standing ovation from the members of the Partido de Conciliación Nacional. Immediately, the orchestra began a selection of patriotic songs until the arrival of the President, when they played the national anthem.

Immediately afterwards, the President began his speech:

Forty years ago, the reds rose up. But we were ready. They began by seizing our sacred lands, by murdering our courageous landholders, by violating our noble women of blue blood. Forty years ago, the Red Devil set foot upon our holy fatherland. But we were ready. The American fleet offered us assistance in an unforgettable gesture of solidarity, but we

---

*   *Leaders of Genius and Iron*

declined it. Because we were ready. Ready to annihilate the hordes of Satan. Ready to rip Bolshevism from our sacred land. Ready to rescue our innocent landholders and their families from the conflagration lit by red demons. They demanded land and we gave it to them –enough to cover their faces until Judgement Day. They demanded food and we gave it to them in lead, the only food that the sons of Lucifer know.

Today, the nefarious hordes of Satan are rising from the grave like zombies. But we are ready. They wish to trick our innocent peasants with promises of beans and tortillas. Their beans are bullets and their tortillas are empty posters. But we are ready. They wish to confuse our naive little brothers, the day laborers with promises of land, even though the only land that the red demon can offer is the grave. But we are ready. They wish to recruit our priests in their dirty war against the impeccable fatherland; even though no one truly consecrated to Jesus would pronounce such blasphemies. But we are ready... But we are ready... A wave of blue will rise up again to drown the red nightmare. Because we are ready!

Neto ate up the President's every word. His face lit up as if he were before Christ Himself at the Sermon on the Mount or if he had found nirvana before the Buddha at the Speech at the Deer Park. Now he felt like one of the chosen.

After finishing his pronouncement against

the evils of equality, people's power, and other satanic ideas, the President greeted his military and civil officers. Meanwhile, the students ate grilled steaks in the main hall until until they were taken by military bus to the Presidential Mansion in San Jacinto, where General Sánchez Hernández himself received the students one by one in his office.

-C'mon in... sit down, kid... So you're a patriot and not one of them red assfucks that wants to drown the fatherland in blood like they did in Russia, China and Cuba where they send you to the firing squad for being a Christian, where they separate babies from their mommas at birth to brainwash them and turn them into soulless robots. If they want blood, blood we'll give them and rivers of blood will wash away the putrefaction from this country. You understand me, kid?

-Yes, General... I mean, mmm, Mister President.

-So you're ready to defend the fatherland against all those who wish to take away everything that by right belongs to us?

-Yes, Mister President!

General Fidel Sánchez Hernández was astonished; he had never seen such a servile face in any buck private or among the most vile suckups and ass-lickers in his cabinet. He was duly impressed by this extraordinary combination of naiveté, greed, fear, courage, servility and pride. He resolved to see what this squalid lad was made of.

-Tell me, kid, where are you from?

-Yes, Mister President... My mother is from

the Departament of Santa Ana and my father was English.

-Your father, English?... Seriously?... I'm asking you seriously... English?

-Yes, Mister President. He left me an inheritance before he died.

-Ah, so he's dead. And what kind of last name is Tecolote?

-It's English, Mister President.

-And what kind of English name is it, kid?

-Mmm, they say it was originally Anglo-Normand, mmm, "de Collette", mmm, and that here, the local yokels couldn't pronounce it correctly, mmm, so then, instead of "hills," it became the name of a bird.

-Kid! You're fucking with me?... I called you in for something serious, see!

- Yes, Mister President.

-And...?

-Yes, Mister President, I'm here to serve the fatherland!

The General put his hand in his pocket, while he moved his head from side to side, not knowing what to think of this kid, so abominably useful for his party. He whipped out two hundred *colones*.

-Here... take it, seems to me that if you're gonna serve the cause, you better get established, y'see.

For the first time in his life, his eyes were completely opened up, thanks to that wad of bills.

-Something to drink?

Neto stood there with his mouth open. He

didn't know what to say. The president of the country, the motherfucker himself, had invited him to drink. Now he felt like a man.

-Since you're a kid, I'm gonna invite you to a bowl of *atol shuco*, unless you want a man's drink.

When he heard the word *shuco*, Neto felt a tremendous urge to heave. He became pallid, he almost fainted when he thought about that liquid with the consistency of phlegm dyed a satanic red. The general felt as if he had put his foot in his mouth.

-Know what...? Since you're now a man, I'm gonna treat you like a man... A bottle of *Gallo*...?

Neto became as red as a beet. He began to tremble with rage. His malevolent eyes reflected the flames of his anger, but only an intelligent and perceptive man such as the General could see it. It was difficult to receive emotions in a face like a stiff tortilla, such as Neto had. He was a born psychopath. He was as ugly and evil as Satan.

-But, what's wrong with you, kid? I'm offering you a drink from one man to another, see.

Neto began stuttering and then he popped the cork.

-It's, it's, it's... It's that I expected a national drink from my President, a patriotic drink, instead of something from a foreign country!

The General jumped to his feet. That brat had brass balls to talk that like to him. He was trying to decide whether to slap him shitless himself or turn him over to Major Roberto so he could practice his interrogation studies when it dawned on him that a man who knew how to hate for such a minimal slight was a man of immense utility.

-You spoke well, kid. I should have flushed that Guatemalan piss down the shitter, but since my boy, General Lucas García, brought it to me as a gift, I didn't want to offend him. Here, I have something for you that is completely national and patriotic, see... just like you, Neto.

That said, he served him a glass of *Tic Tack*. Neto, who had never even so much as sipped a beer, downed it in a single gulp. He felt a fire all the way down to his innards that would burn until the next morning, when flames and smoke would come out his ass. Strengthened, he gave an impeccable military salute to the General and marched out.

The General called his secretary.

-Chabelita!, c'mere... Hurry, get moving.

Right away, a woman with a sinful walk arrived, dressed in a skirt two sizes too small, ridiculously high heels, and a blouse unbuttoned to her navel; all to distract from her bovine face.

-Does my General wish something special to alleviate stress?

As she pronounced these words, she kneeled in front of the General seeking the mouth of his pants with her lips. The President grabbed her by the shoulders and straightened her up pretty damn quick.

-What the fuck... there's work to do, see!

-Yes, General, right away.

-Send all our guests an invitation to serve in the Pro-Fatherland Team for National Salvation. For all that accept, arrange a full scholarship to study at the university. All of them, 'cept that kid that just left.

-Yes, General, right away.

-That kid is very promising, but it seems that he learns evil habits a bit too fast, see. That's why I wanna see him screwed but happy, busy earning a living by the sweat of his brow. Find him a job in a completely useless ministry where he can't fuck up anything important, see.

-What do you have in mind, General?

-Something completely worthless to the country, see... mmmm... Education, yes, that's it, there he can't screw anything up, see.

-Yes, General, right away.

-Something else, it's been a really fucked up day.

-Yes, General.

Chabelita quickly kneeled down and put her lush delicious lips to an infinitely better use.

Solo Flight

I can fly, way up high, in the sky
By and by, with a sigh,
I'll be back in the twinkling of an eye

Noel Wankerman

Neto ran to catch the next bus to Apopa. Although inside he detested his mother for having to earn a living as a humble *shuquera*, he knew he needed someone to cook and wash clothes for him, above all for free. He knew that the quicker he arrived, the happier his mother would be and, maybe she would invite him to eat in a restaurant, something she had only done in key moments in his life –for his first communion, his confirmation, when he received a scholarship to attend the Academy, and when he graduated from high school. He also wanted to arrive while there was still light, so he could see the faces of the lowlifes of the ravine who also made fun of him.

But when he arrived, there was no one waiting for him along the path with open arms and smiling faces, much less orchestras playing in his honor or cheerleaders shouting out his name. He found a handful of people in front of his *champa*, with their heads down. Among them was Father Giovanni Melograno, who just arrived from Montefiascone, a village near Rome. Given that he joined the priesthood only with the purpose of filling his belly and sleeping in a warm, comfortable bed, he gave no importance to the act of learning Spanish and barely knew Latin. To punish his laziness, the arch-bishop sent him to the most miserable shithole in the country.

-Mi dispiace, figlio, tua mamma è morta. Le bendizioni di Dio sia con te. In nome del Padre, il Figlio e...[*]

Neto didn't know what to think. On one hand, he wouldn't have anyone to look after him, but one the other hand, he wouldn't feel the shame of having an illiterate Indigenous mother who sold *shuco*. Now, he could be eve-rything he wanted without having the bother of being associated with that old bat that had only been a drag on his career. Besides, he wouldn't have to share his salary with anyone. He could eat all the chicken he wanted, all alone.

Upon entering the *champa*, he saw Max Alva-rado, the moneylender, praying over the body of Ms Xóchitl Tecolote, *née* Xúchit Tekúlut, seated on the only chair.

-Neto... I am sorry for your loss.

Neto kept quiet. He knew well that don Max's pain was neither emotional not spiritual.

-Neto... she's in a much better place... with-out having to worry about the matters of this world.

Neto could only guess which matters he al-luded to.

-Neto... you're gonna have to do something with your life and you need to get away from

_____

* I'm sorry, son, your mom is dead. The blessing of God be upon you. In the name of the Father, the Son and...

here... Here, there's no future for you and...

Before he could pronounce another word, Neto blurted out:

-300 for the *champa*, not including the furniture.

Max's jaw dropped.

-The truth is... Neto... is that she contracted a loan for 100 *colones*. With interest, that's 200 owe me.

-300 with the furniture, but I keep the books.

-Deal.

Max had never run into such a lucid moneygrubber, so coldblooded and heartless. He gave thanks to the Lord that this man hadn't decided to dedicate himself to work as a money-lender. It seemed unbelievable to him that Neto didn't feel any kind of emotion that was normal for a human being who had just suffered such a loss. His stiff tortilla face never reflected any type of emotion. He was as ugly and evil as Satan.

With 500 *colones* in his pocket, Neto had enough to begin to build his dreams. He had enough to escape from Apopa, to live in a more desirable place such as Acovit, Ciudad Delgado, San Miguelito, El Manguito, Soyapango or Cuscatancingo. But he preferred to invest his money in Apopa where he could get a better house for less money. With this down payment, he built a house with a rose garden, his only vice. He would live in Apopa for the rest of his days.

Lions for Lambs

*I never fear an army of lions led by a lamb,
I fear more an army of lambs led by a lion.*

Alexander the Great

On the following Monday, he presented himself at the Ministry of Education with a letter of appointment. The Minister, Doctor Arquímedes San Goyo, was one of the few people in government respected for his honesty. While the other ministers drove around in Mercedes and Cadillacs, he drove an old Volkswagen –a Beetle so beat up that even the VW emblem had fallen off. It was the only way of running a ministry that received next to nothing. And even if he were a righteous man, the honest truth is that, in any case, there wasn't anything to steal. He took a surprised look at Neto and shook his head.

-I hope you're brighter than you look, kid. With that stupid look on your face, you won't last a week here.

Neto played dumb. He just smiled. He just smiled like an idiot with everyone. And everyone laughed at him. They stuck a paper on his back that said "KICK THE JACKASS TECOLOTE'S ASS." But after a while, they got used to him, nobody paid attention to him at lunch or when he entered the bathroom while they were talking trash about everyone else.

-That motherfucker, San Goyo, is always fucking with me. I swear one day... Ahhhh, hi,

Neto. Just blowing off steam, that's all. Too much work for so few pennies. A man has to think about his family.

After a few months, his colleagues began to see him as a saintly priest confessor. Women told him about their desires and their sexual secrets. Men confided their frustrations in him. They never guessed that evil lurked behind that rigid face. His stiff tortilla face never reflected any kind of sentiment. He was as ugly and evil as Satan. They interpreted his stiffness as a characteristic of a good confident:

-Netito, tell me, What do men really want...?

-Netito, my friend. Would a man really leave his wife for a young colleague like me?

-Neto, tell me. Tell me how I can satisfy the man I love?

-Neto, I've had it up to here with that motherfucker San Goyo. He made me give back the money I got for passing Acovit School. He even made me take back the certification. He gave me this bullshit sermon about serving the people. The poor director... that dyke hag, Julieta Travi, sucked my Tootsie-Pop for nothing... I'm sure it was the first time she ever saw what a man has, ha, ha, ha... Neto, I gotta think about my family. They don't pay us shit...

-Neto, fucker, you gotta help me... Imagine this, I got drunk a few months back and fucked Morsa Bisontina, Carlos's wife... I was drunk. I would've never laid that ass-faced doofette if wasn't truly fucked up. Now she's pregnant and her old man says if she doesn't get an abortion, he's gonna throw her out on the street.

The motherfucker says he had a vasectomy, so it can't be his. That stupid semi-literate bitch don't know how to do nothing. She wants me to get her a fake degree. If I don't, she's gonna snitch on me to wife. Help me out with this, Neto…

Before the year was up, Neto knew all the secrets of MINED: who cheated on their spouse, who hated the boss, who was gay, who took bribes, who were reds and, more importantly, whose floor he had to saw in order to move up. Mysterious, his colleagues' names began to appear in some strange letters.

Dear Mr. Lacayo:
It pains me to inform you that your wife will present herself this Friday at the Auto-Hotel El Castillo at 5:00 in the afternoon in a light blue Toyota in the company of a certain Mr. Otón de la Vara. I know full well what my husband would do to the man who dared take me from his arms.

Advice from a decent woman.
***

Dear General Casanova:
Filthy mouths have libeled your son by declaring he is a frequent visitor of the Pájaro Feliz, an institution dedicated to depravity among men. Although I don't believe for a moment that the fruit of your noble lineage would degrade himself in such a manner, I consider it very important that you hear about the kind of lies that circulate in this cesspool we call society.

A loyal patriot.
***

Excellent Minister:
I pains me to inform you that your office is infested with subversives. It is imperative that you act before this information comes to the ears of

your superiors, or, even worse, the pages of the newspapers. According to my neighbor, the Chief of the Special Directorate of Investigation, these include...

***

Dear Major Roberto:
As a member of the patriot cause, my patriotic duty forces me to denounce the terrorist activities of a certain Otón de la Vara, member of the Cultural Section of the Ministery of Education and known writer of subversive opinions on bathroom walls...

***

El Diario de Hoy, Advertising Section:
Even though there are those who have accused me of subversion, I swear that I have always been a patriot and a Christian and that I have never been a communist or a subversive. Of course, I participated in some pro-union demonstrations and I have family members affiliated with ANDES. In my youth I committed some indescretions by adding my name to manifestos without knowing what I was signing, but the proof of my loyalty is that I am an employee of the Ministry of Education...

***

Mr. Minister:
The situation in Santa Tecla has worsened. Don Melitón Cáceres has always suffered from the bad habit of filling his pockets in every site he visits. Now he has become a rapist. The director of the Acovit School, Ms Travi, told me in private that he forced her to have sex with him and if the Ministry does not remedy the situation, there will be consequences. Given that Ms Travi and her family are highly influential in the Party, it behooves us to demand the resignation of Mr. Cáceres for abuse of power and to compensate Ms Travi. I suggest that we approve a new budget for the school, which is suffering economically. The money they were assigned suddenly disap-

peared... How strange, right?

In a couple of years, Neto found himself the last man in his section. Women were disgusted by him, since every time his long, skeletal finger fell, someone was destroyed. A few women, out of fear or admiration for his malice, arrived ay an accommodation to maintain their posts. Others fled or were fired for denying him his rights. In his boldness, he became more and more misogynous. He told a poor single mother with a child in kindergarten:

-A woman's mouth is only good for two things: to tell me yes or to chomp down on my bud and give me pleasure.

To scientifically ground his position, he made his underlings read the dreams of Irma, one of Sigmund Freud's patients, and her pathological sexual relations with her mouth and he also ordered them to memorize a pseudoscientific treatise that he himself had written: "Cuando una mujer abre la boca: "Lamber, lengüetear, relamer (".* Every woman that worked in his department had to put up with his insanity and submit herself to his inquisition:

Are you married?... Why not?... A woman with a great body like yours will have many possibilities in this section... You'll have to find someone to take care of your children because you're going to work very late with me... Don't worry, I'll give you a ride in my Yugo ... I know a good hotel... All the other say

* *When a Woman Opens her Mouth: Sucking, Tonguing and Resucking*

yes, why do you think you have the right to say no to me?... Either submit to my demands or you'll never have another job in Central America!... We have a list for troublemakers like you who don't want to open their legs!... Bitch, you'll rue the day you were born for making me waste my time!...

The Minister tired of so many anonymous complaints. He began to notice the face of horror and hatred women showed in the presence of the Tecolote. He had survived his fair share of Netos to rise to the position he held. And so, he decided to send him out to supervise special programs in the departments, with the idea that anyone who survived Neto would have a great future in the ministry. With his new position came a salary increase. Dr. San Goyo specifically sent him to the most dangerous zones in the hope that the guerrillas would find him and do the country a favor by executing him. He still had to suffer his visits to the office every Friday. But this change never represented a danger to Neto. He didn't suffer from fear. His stiff tortilla face never reflected any kind of emotion. He was as ugly and evil as Satan.

Radha, the Queen of the Gopis

Radha is the source of all spiritual inspiration.

A.C. Bhaktivedanta Swami Prabhupada

Now that everything was going super-duper-swell for the Ace of Apopa, some women began to pay attention to him, or rather to his wallet. Every time he entered the Gran Auto-Hotel Soyapango with a female underling, he asked the management to play his theme song:

*El cumban-cumban-cumban-chero chero chero
cumbanchero, cumbanchero que se va
el bongo-bongo-bongo-bongo-sero sero sero
bongosero, bongonsero que se va
El casa-casa-casa-Casanova nova nova
Casanova, Tecolote que se va...*

One day, Radomira Bojórquez, the newest and most beautiful woman in the office, began to play telephathy with Neto. She was, without a doubt, one of the most beautiful women Neto had ever seen up close. And so, he signed her contract without reading her file. She was from Chalatenango, and had pale white skin, red hair and green eyes. They say her uncle, a Russian by the name of Radomir Govnoyeddy, was a Soviet agent shot in a mass firing squad along with Miguel Mármol in the thirties, but no one knows for sure. Just that the poor man went out to sell shoes and never returned. They say his eyes were as blue and as wide open as

Siberia and that his kindness had no limits.

Every time Neto looked in her direction, she flashed him a picaresque smile in his direction. He couldn't believe his luck. He asked her for a date and they ended up in the Gran Hotel Paramor on the beach at Majahual. Radomira, or Radha, as everyone called her, showed him a book with all the positions of the *Kama Sutra* and she promised to practice them with him, but with one condition –he had to marry her and quick.

Before the wedding, she showed him her beautiful body but didn't let him touch her. Neto was captivated. He felt like a traveler in the desert, dying of thirst, incomplete for the first time in his life. He held out for three days until he felt like a drunk seated in front of an unreachable bottle of booze. He told her yes, a thousand times yes. They got married that weekend and spent their honeymoon in Acajutla. True to her word, Radha taught him all the thousand positions of the Hindu encyclopedia of love with all her body and soul.

Six months later, she had triplets, blond with blue eyes. They were beautiful girls, too beautiful, and everyone gleefully commented about that behind his back. Radha named them after qualities completely absent in Neto: Esperanza, Caridad y Mercedes and prayed that they turned out the opposite of their putative father. To celebrate the deed, some of his colleagues played Indian music on the office stereo. They gave him a celebration, and served *gallo en chicha, chilate* and *gringas al pastor* with *atol shuco.*

A year later, while he was walking down Calle Arce, Neto stopped to check out the vast selection of pirated films and in the corner of his eye, noticed a DVD box that said *Kama Sutra*. On the cover was Radha with a group of tall, blonde Gringos. She had an enormous penis in each of her orifices and was soaked in a milky liquid that looked like *atol shuco*. He headed over to the DVD stand and discovered that Radha was on the cover of dozens of DVDs, in uncountable sex acts, even with animals and other women: *Las mil y una noches de la Chera Azade (A Thousand and One Nights with Share-a-Twat), Alicia en el país de los mamelucos (Alice in Wonderfuck), Cheras insaciables (Insatiable Babes), Labios lascivos en Lesbos (Lascivious Lips in Lesbos), Bienvenida abordo (Welcome Abord), Rin Tintazo (Rin Tin Twat), Con tía Radha no es pecado (With Aunt Radha it's Not a Sin),* and her masterpiece, a Gringo film with a famous talking horse *--In the Bed with Mr. Ed.* But what most infuriated Neto was when he recognized his former nemeses from his ravine, the kid from the Cock Boys, acting in a film titled *La Granja*, in which Radha took advantage of every beast in the countryside, including the Cock Boys themselves.

Loose tongues in the Salvadoran cinemagraphic industry tell that the famous Serbian director Dragoljub Pizda was just about to recruit her to star in Europe, as the next Cicciolina when he found out she was pregnant.

In spite of being a woman of the "happy life," Radha's career was marked by tragedy, like the overwhelming majority of women in that industry. At fifteen, while she was walking next to the highway to Guarjila with her little sister Tatiana, she ran into a platoon of soldiers who began to gang rape them in the middle of the road. When they were done, they tied Radha's thumbs together and marched her to the barracks in Chalatenango. They left Tatiana behind in a pool of blood. The series of rapes produced a hemorrhage and when she couldn't get up, the sergeant finished her off with a shot to the temple.

In the barracks, the sergeant claimed her as his own property, and enjoyed himself with her all weekend long, until the lieutenant came back. The lieutenant put her in a cell, where he visited her every night until the major discovered her. The major took her to his room there kept her tied to the bed until the colonel got wind of her. The colonel gave her a room in his apartment and a job as a maid. There she washed and ironed his clothes and served as his mistress by night. He kept her like that for a few months, until he was called back to San Salvador. He took her with him and began to take nude pictures of her in various poses, with the idea of selling them to brothels, motels and sleazy dives.

One day, he got hold of a cinematographic camera picked up from a team of Dutch photographers murdered while filming his troops in the act of massacring a whole village. He came up with the brilliant idea of converting Radha into a movie star. Little by little, he found other women and formed a stable of actresses, whom he forced to do the most degrading acts in front of the camera. He and his buds, of course, played all the male roles –at least until growing demand caused them to peter out.

At that point, he sought recruits from among his troops, his friends and even put prisoners in his films, especially when he wanted to make a *snuff film*. Radha only had to witness this once: the man who was riding her began to come. Suddenly, he collapsed and fell on top of her, splattering her with blood and brains. To win a bet, the colonel demonstrated, proof positive, that a man could be coming and going at the exact same moment.

Tecolote, Agent Zero Zero Zilch

I'm a spy, ... in the house of love
I know everything, ... that
you're dreaming of.

Jim Morrison

Dr. Arquímedes San Goyo, in the mean time, tried to eliminate beforehand the danger this man represented. More than any man he had known, he reminded him of Tío Conejo, Uncle Rabbit, the vilest, trickiest, most traitorous, dick-faced motherfucker in the animal world.

He remembered how Tío Conejo tricked all the other animals, until they all went to Tío León, the King of the Jungle, to call a meeting. He did it without advising Tío Conejo, so they could speak openly. But since Tío Conejo was nervous and never slept, he just hopped around endlessly, looking for trouble, and so, he found out about the meeting.

Just like humans, animals have their own protocols, the most powerful sit up front, right in front of the king, while the weakest sit at the edge of the jungle or on a tree limb to keep safe, in case Tío Oso, Tío Tigre or Tío Coyote feel like eating them. But Tío Conejo strolled in like he owned the place and sat right next to Tío León. In those days, rabbits walked upright like human beings and had little ears like muskrats. Tío León's jaw dropped. He asked Tío Conejo:

- You're not afraid of Tío Oso?

- No, why? Haven't you noticed that thanks

to my tricks, that old bear ain't got no tail? I have it in my living room hanging over the sofa. In the summer, I use it to swat flies.

Tío León looked over at Tío Oso, and noticed how red he was blushing from shame.

-Aren't you afraid Tío Coyote will eat you?

-No way, man, I left that poor bastard with broken teeth and a burnt asshole. That Nicaraguan poet José Coronel Urtecho can tell you all about it in verse.

Tío León glanced at Tío Coyote, and saw how he was shitting his pants.

-Aren't you scared Tío Tigre will make a snack out of you?

-Holy damn, you see me trembling? No way, dude, because I don't give a flying fuck about Tío Tigre. You notice how he wears prison stripes? I'm a friend of the judge and that drooler is on parole. One call... and his ass is back in the can.

Tío León looked over at Tío Tigre, and saw him begin to shake.

With all that, Tío León began to worry. If that scrawny piece of shit had that much balls, who knows what he'd be capable of doing. He pointed his finger at Tío Conejo, beckoning for him to draw near.

-I want to share my wisdom with you, Tío Conejo. I'll give you some advice you'll remember the rest of your life. C'mere, closer, closer... That's it... perfect.

He began to rub Conejo's ears to relax him completely. Meanwhile he spoke to him.

-Looky here, my little friend, I'm very impressed by everything you've told me. You've taught me that the battle doesn't always go to the strongest, that the race doesn't always go to the swift, and that laughter doesn't always go to the wittiest.

That said, he firmly grabbed him by the ears, he shook him against the rocks until his ears grew six or eight inches. Then he twirled him over his head like a helicopter. He loosened his grip and let him fly out over the ravine. When he hit the rocks below, he broke his legs and had to hop instead of run. He lost his tail and was left with a little white cotton stump.

San Goyo pondered the story and figured out that he'd have to do the same with that Tecolote before he destroyed the whole ministry. Then he thought about the new educational project aimed at strengthing rural schools with pedagogical resources delivered onsite. To keep from making an enemy out of him, he awarded him with the directorship of a small section of the ministry dedicated to raising educational standard in the least developed departments. Therefore, he sent him to visit schools in the most primitive villages of Morazán, La Unión, Cabañas and Chalatenango. It was a time of all out war, when he had to walk a whole day in, and then another full day out. They even sent him to the islands of the Gulf of Fonseca in a boat full of holes. He had to sleep beneath the rain among clouds of mosquitos, eat moldy tortillas, fight off the horseflies when he had to take a shit and drink water full of parasites. But he never complained, that's how he was raised. He just carried a bottle of *Kitalombriz*, or *Wormaway*, a fine product of the prestigious Laboratorios Dundarelli. He never felt any kind of fear. His stiff tortilla face never reflected any emotion. He was as ugly and evil as Satan. In any case, his new job offered some advantages. He could live off his travel expenses and save his money to buy a car. As an inspector, he demanded pay in kind from every teacher or director. Men had to pay in cash. Some intelligent observers noted that he loved roasted chicken, indeed chicken of any type. That was his favorite dish. So they made sure to keep him well stuffed in bird meat every time he visited the school.

Traveling through the country as an educational consultant strengthened his ties with the Patriotic Team for National Salvation. As a participant in the struggle against subversion, he received 100 *colones* from the *Manus Alba* Foundation for every name he provided. He regularly reported on guerrilla movements in Guazapa, Cabañas, Morazán and Chalatenango. It was then that he took advantage of his new power to avenge himself against the Cock Boys. The young men entered the barracks in Apopa, their thumbs tied with wire, with a mixture of innocence, fear and confusion. They were never seen again by anyone. He conducted an investigation to find the names of the actors who appeared in his wife's films. He sent a list of names of everyone who was not a military officer to his handlers.

Thanks to his everlasting stupid looks, no one suspected anything. Even when he was captured by a guerrilla platoon under the command of his ex-colleague Otón de la Vara in the mountains of Chalatenengo, near San Antonio de los Ranchos, he didn't cough up anything, although they did find a list of names of sympathizers on him. Subcomandante de la Vara, affectionately known as "Sir Oto" for his grand sense of culture and noble nature, ordered his subordinate to interrogate him gently and in great detail, as befit a gentleman of his class. He had his men tie him naked to a chair with a hole in the bottom, so the guys could kick his nuts in an effort to loosen his tongue.

-You spying son of a bitch! Where did you get that list?

-They're students.

-What do you mean they're students, you shit-faced cop?

-The director of San Benito School gave it to me.

-For what purpose?

-They're kids who attend school there.

-And why do you collect the names of school boys? Are you ass-fucking pedophile?

-To calculate the Ministry's budget.

-Find that buttfuck principal. We'll see who comes to justice tonight.

Neto kept completely calm while they brought in the principal. When he arrived, he shouted out a greeting.

-Don Manuel, we see each other again. Tell me, why did you tell me they were students?

The director was completely perplexed. He had no idea why they brought him there. They showed him the list. Terror never marked Neto's face, he was a psychopath by vocation, and that saved his life. His stiff tortilla face never reflected emotion. He was as ugly and evil as Satan.

-What's that?

-It's a list.

-Of what? Are they your students?

-No. of course not.

-Then, who are they?

-I don't, I don't, I don't know. I've never seen those names in my life.

-You don't know? And you live around here? You really don't know?

-No, I don't know, I don't know, I don't know...

And then, a shot was heard.

-Untie that other piece of shit and let him go.

The subcomandante looked at Neto.

-Get your ass outta here or I'll give you a bullet for the fun of it.

-My clothes... Can I pick up my clothes?

-You have 10 seconds. One second more and you'll be dressed in lead.

Neto ran to pick up his clothes, he let them fall upon the document and picked it up in the confusion. Her began to run. He ran and ran without stopping, not even to put on his clothes. He arrived in Chalatenango bare-ass naked, with his clothes and the list in his hands, completely scratched all over by thorns and insect bites, his bare body covered in mud and sticker burrs. He kept running till he reached the barracks. Upon seeing him, a soldier aimed an M-16 at him. Neto threw himself on the ground and begged for his life.

-Don't shoot, don't shoot. I have important

information on the subversives. Very important, very important.

The soldier was about to squeeze the trigger when an officer stepped out.

-What's going on here? What is this shit?

-Captain, my captain. I just escaped from the terrorists. I have a list of sympathizers. Listen to me, my captain!

After hearing his story, they gave him time to wash up and get dressed. They took him to Military Headquarters in the capital. There they waited for him with great anticipation. But when they saw how stupid he looked, they felt like shooting him then and there. Only after confirming who he was, they let him go free, but not before lending him to Major Roberto, who used him for a few hours as a taekwando dummy, to the beat of the musical theme of the film *Rambo*, starring Silvester Stallone. The Major tried out jabs, hooks, uppercuts, kicks, throws and finger jabs to the eyes. Strangely, Neto didn't flinch. His stiff tortilla face didn't reflect any emotion. He was as ugly and evil as Satan. Major Roberto's special antennae were activated in the act, "Hmmm... It seems this guy is one of my team and to honor this, I'm gonna give you a chance not to get scorched." With the uncommon strength of his arms, his lifted him up high and dropped him on his forehead.

-Looky here, shitbird, I done sniffed you out. And we're gonna talk bare assed... Bare assed is how we're gonna talk.

Neto's eyes lit up. "A man...!" he thought. "he wasn't on my list, but we're not talking of any old man. Though I could go through a lot... And my dignity? To Hell with that! The illustrious history of the Roman Empire is full of great characters who put up with kicks, punches, headbutts and other sacrifices."

-I know what you're thinking, shitbird. But don't flatter yourself. You're not my kind. But I detest that psychopath face you're wearing. As stiff and terribly disgusting as a badly made tortilla. But don't you worry, cause in honor of your psychopath blood, I'm gonna apply our code of honor. You choose between two things: Number one, you can die like a human torch, like the scorched tecolote that you are, or Number two, "erase and start all over again." Forgiving and forgetting on your part. Total amnesty, that is.

Elevated in evil, Neto felt transported to an imaginary world. He felt a profound admiration for that man, for his cold blood, for his brutality and, above all, for the cynical way he treated him like a friend. Neto would have given anything to be Major Roberto, and in a moment of brain fever, he was transported to the poorest hamlets of the country. He saw himself converted into Major Roberto, and even Sylvester Stallone, running down trails while he wiped Suchitoto, Las Hojas, La Joya, Tenango, Guadalupe, El Mozote, El Sumpul, Copapayo, etc., off the map. But he didn't thirst for human blood. He imagined himself firing an M16, a grenade launcher, a rocket launcher, and other artifacts of war against all the chicken coops in the country, from the smelliest and most rustic, to the most technological, such as El Gallo Picudo, Corporación Huevos y Valor, La Cresta d'Oro, Aves S.A. In his feverish hallucinations, he imagined that the blood of 75,000 birds was concentrated in a thick thread of blood. The thread extended through restaurants, kitchens, markets, parks, workshops, town squares, bridges, hills, highways, mountains and rustic trails until it emptied into the Lempa, Sumpul, Paz and Goascorán rivers, and even beyond the nation's borders. The entire nation would look on terrified. The meteorological center would become alarmed upon registering bizarre climate changes such as tempests of chicken beaks, feet, combs, innards and feathers. Meanwhile, Major Roberto was becoming impatient. He'd never seen a poor devil with such a stupid face.

-Turdling. I'm waiting for your answer.

Neto came down from his chicken storm, and as he licked the Major's army boots, he exclaimed: "Whatever you wish, your majesty. Whatever you wish, your majorness. Whatever you wish, your excellency."

The Major gave him a kick that finished off his last real teeth. In later years, his false teeth would add even more rigidity to his face. Try as he may, he could never muster any noble sentiments as he pronounced his hackneyed speech on "the poor children of the countryside." His stiff tortilla face never showed emotion. He was as ugly and evil as Satan.

Major Roberto presented him with honors before the members of the military high command. "Yes, I like this kid, y'see. Yes, of course, this kid has nationalist fiber. He's got a tough presence, ay . . ." He exclaimed enthusiastically while he held him in his arms, trying to keep him on his feet. Blood gurgled out of him. Red strings of blood hung like threads from his drool-ard mouth. The scene disturbed those present. The military officers hearkened back to a remote primogenital time, when fire, the sparks from the anvil, the open skies of purple and gold, the sweat of heroes and, above all, majestic rivers of red blood flowed turbulent, wide and deep over the fertile fields that sustain us, over the foundations of primitive sand, over the ancestral, free and evidently Creole sand that always and forever will be impregnated with the sacrosanct and redeeming scarlet flow. With the immolated and thick blood, sanctified, sacrosanct, sadistic and satanic symbol of national sovereignty, under the Alianza Republicana Nacionalista, that so many times has glorified and anointed with red the maternal breast of the fatherland. None of those present repressed the lament and flush with infinite emotion, struck up the march of the Alianza Republicana Nacionalista:

Alianza Republicana Nacionalista of El Salvador
Alianza Republicana Nacionalista of El Salvador
Present, present for the fatherland
Liberty is written in blood,
Labor with sweat.
We unite sweat and blood,
But first El Salvador.

When in our beloved fatherland strange voices were heard...
The nationalists surged forth thus proclaiming

Fatherland yes, communism no,
Fatherland yes, communism no,

Alianza Republicana Nacionalista of El Salvador
Present, present for the fatherland
Liberty is written in blood,
Labor with sweat.
We unite sweat and blood,
But first El Salvador.

Tremble, tremble, communists!
El Salvador will be the tomb where the reds are
finished.
Thus saving all América, our immortal América.

The ministry gave Neto a few weeks to recover in the Military Hospital. And when all was said and done, the list was filed and no one even looked at it until after the peace treaty. When they finally saw the information it contained, they realized they could have eliminated the entire leadership of the Frente Farabundo Martí para la Liberación Nacional.

His old benefactor, General Sánchez Hernández used his influence to find him a new job at Estudiantes Salvadoreños y Trabajadores Aliados Federación Autónoma, S.A. (ESTAFASA), a privatized organization created to administer international educational aid from the Collosus of the Frozen North. Since there was ample opportunity to enrich himself by adjusting sums and losing receipts, this was the chance he had waited for his whole life long

Book III:
Maturity, Full Powers and the Decline of Neto

People try to put us down
Just because we get around
Things they do look awful cold
Yeah, I hope I die before I get old
The Who

I hope you're on vacation or you have a long weekend or you called your boss with your most anguished, hoarse, stuffed up voice, telling about the thirty thousand pains in your belly, to tell him, of course, you're going to the ISSS –Importa Satanás Su Salud (To Hell with Your Health); that even though all the lights are on and the curtains open to let in the bright morning sunshine, that everything looks black. This always works for me in the good old US of A. Once, my boss even threw a farewell party for me cause her cousin, my doctor, told her I was about to die. But here I am, alive and wagging my tail.

You're gonna need some time, cause you've just finished the appetizers and the salad. Now comes the best fucking steak of your life, Texas sized. Take a short break every hour. Move your ankles, elbows and knees in a circular motion once an hour to avoid blood clots. If you got a cooler, fill it up *Pilseners*, none of that *Gallo* or *Salvavidas* piss, cause this is a Salvadoran book, written in Cuscatancingo, specifically for Salvadorans. If you're overseas, I don't give a fuck what you drink. Have some ham and cheese sandwiches with mustard close by. Toast the bread without burning it. In the middle of your reading, it's gonna do you good –the next best thing to a good fuck.

Now Neto has arrived in the twenty first century and all his actions are more or less coetaneous –look up that motherfucker if you don't know what it means. You gotta remember that Neto ain't alone in his adventure. You gotta meet his cronies to see them for what they are. And if you work with similar scumbags, add these names to the gang of Maritornes, Celestinas, el Huasón, Tecolote and other examples of subhumanity that infest your office.

Stultifera navis

Yeah, climb on board
Ship's gonna leave ya far behind
Climb on board
Ship of fools, ship of fools.

Jim Morrison

At ESTAFASA, they bumped him up to section chief in charge of supervising teachers. They provided him with a new office with a panoptic view of all his subalterns and a swivel chair so he could focus his Tecolote gaze on all the young women. Another advantage his office provided was venetian blinds, to provide him with discretion during his "chat" with new female employees. Some of them went in with red lips and came out with white.

The Adversary continued to labor to fulfill the pact that Neto signed. One fine morning, Netiyo the businessman lunched upon the wonderful news that he would administer a brand new national program based on new pedagogical foci. That, at least, was the official story. Voices in the foreign community maintained that the true purpose was political proseletization in certain key departments during the upcoming election. That way, he could kill two birds with one stone. The program would be funded by a nefarious agency from a certain frozen country and he would come into millions, whose count could never be known with exactitude. As Ferdinand and Isabel said, "Tanto monta, monta tanto (Such an amount, amounts to so much)." Neto claimed twenty million, in the countryside they claimed six million, and for the poor subalterns, the claim was barely two million. The truth was never known, what's certain is that taking into account the quality of his administration, the famed performance of his team (without forgetting the quantity of bribes he handed out to shut up any snitches) he probably spent less than a million. Neto was an expert in the art of these truculencies. He only needed a brilliant bookkeeper with a hard face and enough aces up his sleeve to make ghost figures appear or change seven figures into four or viceversa.

During his tenure at MINED he had a bitter experience with his bookkeeper. Poisonous and obsessive as a scorpion –indeed, his sign was *Scorpio*. Neto had turned on his radar to discover what made a bookkeeper tick who always refused to fold, due to his whims of honesty, decency, for manhood. How he hated those words! They formed no part of his semantic field, and neither did the word "human." With no remorse in his putrid head, Neto fabricated false information and revealed a terrible secret to the directorate of MINED. He cynically pressured them, very sure that the high honchos would not want a subversive infiltrator, an active collaborator in urban guerrilla warfare. Every time he remembered that deed, a triumphant smile marked his face. His psychopathic nature did not allow him to feel like normal people and he only found pleasure in the pain of his fellow man. He never had mercy. Whenever he made a subaltern suffer, his face of stiff tortilla showed full satisfaction. But it was a strange smile, a kind of mocking look on a stone demon. He was as ugly and evil as Satan.

The ground was sowed to extend his poison. In the second week of his directorate, he received two fabulous notices: the general director of the program and the administrative bookkeeper retired. Neto spilled over in worms. That is, from a very worm-like pleasure because he had the opportunity of contracting a gusana, that is a woman named Susana Gusana, who let him make and unmake at his desire, and whom we will speak about later on. What a great slice she was going to serve. . . . After that, he looked for an accountant. He got to work interviewing five hundred professionals with reknowned careers, experts in the field of finance, and finally, he settled on an ignorant, repugnant, fussy shit-kicker with a face like a winch. This last quality truly called Neto's attention, but what really motivated him to hire him was his tenure as general manager of various chicken factories, such as the *Cresta d'Oro* and *Gallinas Turulecas SA*. Neto thought of taking advantage of his ample experience with chickens to initiate, once and for all, a demonic, bloody and clandestine war against all subject of that foul smelling race of fowls. With maximum authority over the project, it was incumbent upon him to select the new director, that is, his new coordinator. But he would do this slowly and thoughtfully in order to continue as the true power behind the supreme director. Indeed, this is how he signed the letters he sent to his subalterns: Neto, el supremo.

The second step to victory was to form a

bold, quarrelsome, team of Mafiosi that didn't give a fuck about anything. He needed bullshitters, specialists in blowing smoke up people's asses to distract the focus of attention while he robbed them out the asshole. The bullshitters had a green light to make life hard for those who really worked and those who had the stones to discover the tremendous tamale pie cooked up by Neto.

"Fuck 'em, fuck 'em" –he told them- turn 'em into nothing, . . . make cunts outta 'em, stalk 'em, drive your workmates and rural instructors nuts. Make 'em lose hope, martyr 'em. Don't even give 'em time to think. And don't sweat if somebody complains about you. It ain't gonna bust my balls. I'm the one who'll bail you out.

The third step would be to justify it all with theoretical bases for all his. "Pedagocial strategies without foundation are like kitchen recipes".

Little by little, Neto developed his leadership principles, based on the German efficiency of the famous *Führerprinzip*. With these, he indoctrinated them, above all, his team of con men, his group of pedagogues, or rather, pedagogical jokers who were ready for any kind of scam that saved their job at ESTAFASA. Outside that institution, they wouldn't have had a chance because most of them were petulant fools who would be lucky to have a degree from a garage university.

A few authentic pedagogical inspectors from MINED verified a lot about the dirty goings on in the corrupt quarters of ESTAFASA, and they constantly complained anonymously. It was no

secret to anyone that Neto received a higher salary than the MINED inspectors. It was no secret to anyone that even the instructors in the
rural areas had better academic training than
many of the clowns such as Juli Travi, Brenda,
Morsa Amorfa, or la Pirulis, who were hired by
ESTAFASA. The rural instructors threw in the
towel, deciding to retire from the project or keep
silent. There were a few who, from time to time,
complained about the abuses committed by
the people of ESTAFASA, but since in the rural
areas, anyone could have someone murdered
for a minimal cost of five dollars, they sent out
anonymous letters of complaint to the project director who cynically replied: *"As long as
school instructors make out no formal complaints
against Juli Travi or the others, there is nothing
I can do."*

On Neto's face there was a triumphant
smile every time his boss blurted out such ir-
responsible and frivolous exhortations. "What
an ice-cold woman!" "How easy it is shut her
snout with a free ticket to damned spa!" Not
even Pontius Pilate himself . . . Nor even same
old Judas himself . . . At least Judas sold himself more dearly than that Susanita, that tripled
distilled concentrate of Cuban gusano worms,
who never flinched when sacrificing the rural
teachers of El Salvador, who never sweat about
eradicating the mistreatment meted out to the
poor instructors who naively believed in a quality program instilled in political change. They
were just another toy for the agencies of power.
For them, once a month it was torture to receive those assistants who dared to scream at

them, publicly humiliate them, to practice bald face intrigues to ruin their interpersonal relations, to ask what political party they belonged to, use them to transport proseletizing political material from the ruling party and, worst of all, divulged school's secrets to the four winds. Naively, they asked for help from Neto or that selfsame Susanita, but they were conformed by hearing the same old repetitive response in her falsetto voice, from that false cupie doll: "as long as the rural instructors fail to make formal complaints, there is nothing I can do. I'm not going to lose sleep, especially over something like this. Besides, you need to check with Neto, not me. If not, let him do my work and let me do his." The rural instructors just smiled but said in private: "What a disgrace of a woman! What a disgusting gusana worm!"

With these responses, Neto had a green light to give free rein to his plans. He never made a mistake: hiring that selfsame Susanita was a bullseye. Even she had to memorize his sage doctrine. Here are the most relevant point, which appear in his book, *Priniciples of Leadership for Men of Genius and Steel:*

1. Where to aim your boot.

He proclaimed he was going to leave you in peace, but like a good scorpion, he just bid his time for the right moment. He boasted of having provoked various firings. Later, he slowly pressed down with his boots because knowing where to put them is an exquisite and delicate art. The troglodite puts them in a kettle, but the trained expert gifted with artistic genius has something infinitely more subtle in store.

As the great martyr against Bolshevism, the distinguished Doctor Dan Mitrione explained, "The right pain, at the precise moment, in the precise quantity, for the desired effect." While Dan Mitrione stated that "Above all else, you have to be efficient. You have to cause the pain that is strictly necessary, not a millimeter more. We must control our emotions, in any case. You must act with the efficiency of a surgeon and with the perfection of an artist."

2. Panoptic vigilance.
Like the tecolote, a bird that sees all from its perch on the tree top or on top of an electricity pole, you must constantly make a visual map of the terrain to find out if everything is in place and attack every out of place movement. I have you all well marked down on my grid. You haven't even noticed that I eyeball you and have my ear on you at every moment. From my little window, I see who comes to work late, who dresses shabbily, who come in with a hangover and for that I don't have to sniff out the oaf. From my panoptic window I see everything. Sometimes I don't say a thing. But this is just to make aware that my omniscient tecolotic eyes gaze upon everything. And never forget that here the walls have ears. We have microphones in all the offices, in all the halls, even in the bathrooms. As a great British philosopher once said, "A state of permanent awareness and vigilance ensures the automatic functioning of power". Never forget: *de omnibus dubitandum!*

3. Make your work known.

Before becoming Educational Project Chief, everyone made fun of me. They used to call me *aguacate* meaning according to Jim Casalbe's *Puro Guanaco*: avocado, shitkicker. Since nothing occurred to me, I brought out another version called *The Other Side of the Avocado*. In both books I proposed the steps to establish a state of law and order through education –a tecolotic state of pure vigilance. Thanks to constant and generous grants from the *Manus Alba* Foundation, these books were able to see the light of day. After that, nothing came to mind, and for that reason, I had to associate with other authors such as Edward Wilson, Bill Sullivan, Sam Murach, Phillip Allen, Lee Pace y Ray Brocco from the Good Shepherd/Puzzle Palace Press of Langley, Virginia. I also had the opportunity to be co-author with experts at the DINA Press of Chile under the aegus of Augusto Pinochet, who treated me like a little nephew during his visit to Cuzcatlán, and to tell the truth, I admired him for his philosophy, his charisma and the tenderness with which he treated the people of Chile, above all, all the artists and musicians. That man was a sweetheart. From him, I learned the smile, the sweetness and the delicate treatment he showed to his subalterns. He taught me his motto, --the apt saying, *"faber est suae quisque fortunae."*

4. The anti-Hipocratic Oath.

Use your talents to advance yourself, not for the good of others. Psychology is a strong tool for studying others' weaknesses and to provoke them into falling into error. As a professional psychologist, I make good use of error and collect information to communicate and adapt the mind to the tecolotic state we wish to construct. I'm not joking. To advance in the workplace, you must have everyone else fighting among one another like a bucket of crabs. As pedagogical consultants, you must teach these strategies in schools. Children must learn these competencies in order to be effective communicators in the future tecolotical society. Communication can serve to clog up the flow of information. It's true that we depart from the text to foment correct reading and writing in the schools. It's an order of the new millenium that children read. But be careful! Literature must incite the masses to hate those who attempt to construct a state based on equality. We are not equal and the world has to know why –all Glory to the Fourteen Families. That's why you must fulfill your role to insure that instructors implement correct techniques and tools to create compentent readers and writers, but never hack writers with naïve ideas of subversion.

5. No one leaves ESTAFASA.

Here we're family and anyone who spills the family jewels will be punished, and will have no future and will rue the day we were betrayed. Women: "Loose lips sink ships." Your lips only serve to render pleasure to men, not to leave them shipwrecked. Do not open your mouths for anyone outside ESTAFASA. Men: your only reliable buddy is the one between your legs. Don't trust any other. This order is non-arguable. Nothing leaves ESTAFASA.

6. Claw out the road of traitors.

We fire traitors. And here Susana Gusana will have to excuse me. Because, even if she promises good references, I never comply with those who are fired. I will never comply. Let that remain clear! I have become the bird of ill omen in the shade of a tecolote that darkens their careers forever. Wherever they go, my beak will pursue them. I'm gonna screw'em all with horrible references. And any severe infraction will be punished with much more. Write down the address of any suspected colleague, write down the address of their families, write down the names and addresses of their buds. Everyone will know the vengeance of the Tecolote.

7. Never forget that education is only a façade.

We're here for the noble ideal of serving the Fatherland. And that way, we give a better future to the poor children of the school sunken in misery. Everything is related. But if you don't understand me, I'm going to evoke the glorious words of the Major. As he said on various occsasion, "If we're gonna speak bare-assed, then bare-assed we're gonna speak". Our true mission is to erradicate the reds, be they fathers of families, instructors, directors or even mere janitors of rural schools, which we so badly serve. And I'm not going to repeat this again. We are giving a quality service, to strengthen language that will serve to communicate in an effective manner in the new nationalist state. We are writing a new page in national history. We are making history for a different society, with human sense. You are not mere pedagogical technicians. You are carrying out the words of our immortal Major: "Patria sí, comunismo no! "

To better understand how my principles work, it behooves us to consult the greatest authority on this subject; Joseph Goebbels, a propaganda genius. Some famous principles propelled his work. Today, they are used as tools of propaganda. Here they are, so you may learn:

1. Simplication and focus on a single enemy. Adopt a single idea, a single symbol, a single enemy.

2. Method of contagion. Paint all your enemies with the same brush.

3. Projecting. Accuse your adversary with your own errors or defects, answering an attack with an attack. If you can't deny bad news, invent other news to distract. . . . And in that, Juli Travi is an expert. She can blow smoke up anybody's ass.

4. Exageration and disfiguration. Convert any anecdote, as small as it may be, into a grave threat.

5. Vulgarization. All propaganda must be popular, its level adapted to the most moronic individual to whom it is directed. The greater the audience to be convinced, the lesser the mental effort effected. The receptive capacity of the masses is limited and their comprehension is even less, besides, they have a great ability for forgetting.

6. Orchestration. Propaganda must be limited to a small number of ideas repeated constantly presented once and again from dif-

ferent perspectives but always converging on the same concept. Without breaks or doubts. If a lie is repeated enough time, it will become the truth.

7. Renovation. You must constantly emit new information and discussions with rhythms such that by the time the adversary responds, the public is already interested in something else. The adversaries' responses must never arrest the crescendo of lies.

8. Verisimilitude. Construct arguments from different sources, through so-called sound bites or fragmentary information.

9. Silencing. Shut down all questions about those who have no arguments and dissimulate all news that favors the adversary with the help of allied means of communication.

10. Transfusion. As a general rule, propaganda always operates through a preexisting substrate, be it a national mythology or a complex of traditional hatred and prejudices; it deals with spreading arguments that can take root and grow into primitive attitudes.

11. Unanimity. Convince the mob to think "like everyone else," creating a false impression of unanimity.

-And in many of these principles, Julita Travi is an expert, a true hostis humani generis. Let's see, Juli... would you like to share your experiences in the field, at the schools, with those present.

-Well, I can only ssay that on one of the tripss I had to walk a long way. The ESTAFASA vehicle couldn't enter becauss it was flooded with mud. And I told the driver, "Oh no, don Chicho, I'm going in no matter what." And I go along and stepped into some mudholess becauss I was watching the birdiess high up in some concaste trees. And since I was in high heelss and all tarted up, I sunk in quickly. Then I went and, with all my might, I got my tootsies out. But bad luck made me fall on a rock then and there. Ooh, I broke a toe nail. . . Looky here, I have a toe nail misssing. And what hurts most is that I had them all dolled up by a teacher during a formation in Cabañas. I took her out of the formation and all morning long, she painted my nails. She is an artist.

People mumbled about her strange dis-course. Some of those present such as Frasquito and Ricardo affirmed that only she alone could give certain twists to her strange discourses, but no one else noticed. The Tecolote, for his part, watched her in ecstasy. With a smile from ear to ear, he never found a way of dissimu-lating enough Travi's brilliant discourses. And, making a tecolotic effort to contain his emotion, he only remarked to her:

-Oh, how much I admire you. What great competencies you have, woman, what great competencies you...

And so, in this way, *asinus asinum fricat.*

Who's Afraid of the Big Bad Wolf, the Big Bad Wolf, the Big Bad Wolf?

Who's afraid of the Big Bad Wolf
Big Bad Wolf, Big Bad Wolf
Who's afraid of the Big Bad Wolf
Tra la la, not me!

Frank Churchill & Ann Ronell.
From the film *The Three Little Pigs*

Taking into account his experiences up in the mountains, his superiors took care to only send him to cities firmly under government control. But this didn't mean he was completely free of problems. While he was supervising teacher training at Maximiliano Hernández Martínez School in Izalco, he heard that certain sound that always enraged him.

-Cock-a-doodle-doooooooo!

-What the hell's going on here? Is this a school or a goddamn farm?

He stuck his head out the window and a cock rooster lunged at his face. He grabbed it threw it to the ground, but its spurs tore the legs of the old, wornout pants he was wearing, scratching his thigh, leaving his leg dripping with blood. He stomped the cock rooster until only feathers were left. When he left the room, everyone looked at him in horror.

-Don Neto, what happened to you? Are you okay, don Neto? Do you want us to take you to the doctor?

He looked at his leg and almost fainted.

-I-i-it was a dog. I mean... a wild dog, bigger than a *cadejo* devil dog, it jumped through the window and attacked me.

The director sent the teachers out to look for the dog, but they didn't find anything, just a dead cock rooster and blood all over the place.

-We didn't find anything, but look, it killed our school mascot, the last living descendent of General Maxilimilano Hernández Martínez's fighting cock. It must have been a wolf to do what it did.

On the back ESTAFASA, his subaltern, la Pirulis, tried to break the ice, as always, with the same old story.

"Don Netooooh, y'know why I love my husband sooooo much?" Neto felt his blood boil and yelled out in a state of frenzy.

-I don't have a fucking idea. Go grab General Hernández Martínez's dead cock so he'll do you the favor.

-Ay, don Netooooh. I was just trying to break the ice. It's just that my husband leaves me so alone. He's a poor sap that doesn't want to study. He wants to live off selling *atol shuco*. Imagine that!

-He's a faggot, a buttfuck like no other. You'd better find some other poor fucker as soon as you can.

After saying that, he convulsed into the same rage and began foaming at the mouth. The chauffeur stopped at an empty field and la Pirulis rubbed him with rue, slapped him with aloe and a handful of sticks until he regained consciousness. They recommended that he go to the hospital but he refused completely.

-I pay taxes. I'm a nationalist and an authentic servant of the Fatherland. That's why I must go wherever the poor are.

Tired of his bullshit, they dropped him off at a government clinic. Once there, he had to wait all day to be attended to. At first, he tried to use his influence as friend of former president Fidel Sánchez Hernández, and of the current Minister of Education Doctor Arquímedes San Goyo, but that got him nowhere with old school mean faced nurse, who pushed him to the end of a line made up of women who were waiting for vaccinations for their children. The doting mothers, with their wisdom and instinct for preservation, which was translated into advice for staying alive, intuited that this bird of ill omen who had nested in a government clinic –an option created only for people with meager resouces—would put their babies in jeopardy due to his halitosis, his black aura and his evil tecolote eyes. They pulled out their amulets against the evil eye. They covered up their children, even though many of them had high temperatures. A nurse passed by and warned them about this.

-These babies have a temperature of over a hundred and three, ladies. They're expiring.

The women demanded that the old tecolote leave:

-Don't you see the evil bird that just nested here. That old guy has the bucks to go somewhere else.

-Well, he has just as much right as any other

Salvadoran to be attended by the clinic. He'll just have to wait until we've finished with everyone else.

Seeing they couldn't do anything to get him thrown out of the place, they decided to scare him out if his wits. And so, they all began to chant:

"Ill formed Tecolote, who sings all his life, sing me the praise of the Immaculately Conceived Woman."

Stunned by all this mumbo jumbo, he decided to move over to a corner of the adjoining room from where he could monitor the pace of the line. He was puzzled that there was only a single woman there. It was a mother, with beautiful blond tresses who held a baby in her arms. Neto didn't hesitate to tecolotolize her.

-If this hen looks good from the back, no doubt she'll look better from the front. I'm going to charm her with my tecolotic subtlety.

Trying to be cute, he caressed the beautiful blonde hair and approached with his owl-like beak to smell the odor. The bold tecolote let loose an insinuating lascivious moan from his unplumed head. And at that precise instant, he discovered that he was dealing with a man waiting on his wife. All the color drained from Neto. The offended party looked like a macho, repulsive, hellbent gangster with a slight touch of Hulk Hogan. Neto recognized him. He was the professional wrestling champion who used to put on shows at the Arena Santanita. Without thinking twice, he landed a terrible punch in Neto's gut. Various hours later, he awoke with his stomach inflamed and the news that they had given him his first rabies shot. The next few days were hell. Neto sent out the janitors and secretaries for ice cubes because he couldn't stand the inflammation in his stomach. He could have assuaged the torture with a bit of honesty, instead of heroically enduring the rabies shots. In an attempt to theoretically justify his conduct, he insistently consulted *National Geographic,* leading himself into tremendous self-deception: "Advanced scientific research has demonstrated that no bird can carry rabies." Perhaps that's why he never recognized the truth that bled at his unconscious and his ripped gut, he was never bitten by a dog. Do you understand? Imagine a bird! He was never bitten by a dog, but by a stupid, bold and unlucky bastard of a fighting cock!

The news reached fever pitch. In Sonsonate, the authorities emitted an alert warning about a ferocious rabid female dog that supposedly ran free down the highways and dusty lanes. For several weeks, on public radio, at the schools, at departmental headquarters, and at teacher training sessions, everyone was dee-lighted to hear a strange and amusing story called "Neto's Bitch."

Days of Wine and Roses

*The days of wine and roses laugh and
run away like a child at play
Through the meadow land toward a closing door
A door marked 'Nevermore,' that
wasn't there before.*

Henry Mancini

Collige virgo rosas!

At ESTAFASA, Neto was received as a hero.
They suspended activities for the day to honor
him with a showing of the English film, *Chicken
Run*, to commemorate his ethnic background.
There was *atol shuco* for everyone. Fortunately,
no one could see his face in the dark, all purple with rage. He cracked his teeth and made
fists with his knuckles until he felt an unknown
hand in his crotch. With his fingers, he followed
the hand to the arm and thence to the body of
Merchita Mogollón, his secretary.

In spite of her forty years, Merchita had a
great body and to feed her nine children, she
was capable of anything and experienced in
almost everything. She kept her great shape
by dancing at the Club XTC every Saturday
at six in the afternoon. Thanks to her striped
belly, they called her the "star-retch mark" of
the show. She was well known for her pugilistic
abilities. She boxed with her huge breasts, jab-
bing spectators in the face with a right tit and
then immediately crossing with a left. Her claim

to fame was to march around the stage shadowing boxing her breasts like Muhammad Ali. She also mastered the art of picking up tips with her vulva. Spectators would leave a stack of quarters some eight inches high and Merchita would swallow them up with her cunt like a vacuum cleaner. She dropped them in a box and came back for more.

And later, if the audience was lucky, the real show began. The owner only had enough to bribe the porkers once, twice a week or so, so Merchita could only do her thing 5 or 10 times a month. She began with a sexual *Vaudeville* sexual, passed through the plant kingdom, experimenting with celery, cucumbers, bananas and carrots. One of the highlights of the night was "Who is stronger: Man vs. Carrot," in which she counted how many men her colleagues could accommodate while she pleasured herself with a single carrot. If, by this moment the police hadn't arrived, she put the carrot aside and advanced to the next step –sucking the Tootsie-Pop of goats and burros. Once she tried it with a horse but the damn critter soaked her face and hair. Finally she offered the carrot to the public and anyone who dared eat the whole carrot got her for the night. When Neto was there, they always passed it to him. And good old Neto chomped it down like Vitamin Z.

This time, Neto had no illusions. He was still married to Radha and helped out economically with the triplets. He didn't get a divorce because he wasn't going to let other woman make a fool out of him. And, despite all else, he felt more and more attracted to the triplets. When Esperanza, the most daring one, got knocked up when she was fourteen, he received the baby as if it were his own. And, indeed, after a few months, it began to look more and more like him, the Tecolote mug, the same hunchback, the same ugliness, the same stupid look: something that neighbors and colleagues who ran into him at La Tiendona quickly picked up on. One day, an anonymous colleague left a DVD of *Chinatown* on his desk.

Merchita would never be more than a toy. But just as you have to take care of a toy, he took care of Merchita. He passed her coin to buy better clothes. He bought her rings at the Mercado Ex-Cuartel. He brought her roses from his garden. When he had to travel, he took her with him to take notes and share his bed in the Lenca Skank-Ho Motor Inn in San Miguel, the Auto-Hotel Victorioso in San Vicente, The Motel Santaneca Feliz in Santa Ana and the Love Garden Hotel in Santa Rosa. Always attentive to the ladies, in the bus station he invited her to a dinner of coffee and Olocuilta-style pupusas.

The Rose without Petals

"Yo no estoy en un lecho de rosas"

Rubén Darío

Merchita loved roses and Neto did what he could to bring her one everyday. He had planted his whole patio with various types of fine roses in blazing colors and sensual fragrances. A *parfumier* would have considered him a genius for his mastery of fragrances.

One day, however, a new neighbor arrived, his lifelong enemy, Otón de la Vara. The economic situation confronting all literary professionals in El Salvador obliged him to seek refuge in a hovel in Apopa surrounded by gangsters, which only tecolotic and somber spirits, such as Neto, could consider a paradise.

When Otón discovered who lived next to his new house, he resolved to avenge himself for all the evil that the Tecolote had done to him. As a distinguished hero of the guerrilla uprising and leader of the much celebrated Final Offensive, in which he and his boys surrounded and frogmarched the famous Green Berets out of the old Sheraton Hotel in their underwear, he wasn't afraid of the devil himself. As a cultural figure, endowed with a magnetic personality, he had the adulation –or at least the envy-- of all the nation's writers and artists. He converted his new house into the scene of a never-ending *tertulia* of the arts. But he also took care to teach a moral lesson to his neighbor. He bought every animal he could and taught them to howl all night in a chorus. Since he was a Bohemian and a literary critic, he worked all night and slept during the day. So he invited all his buds to come and party big time every night and pointed out Neto's door as the neighborhood vomitory and urinal.

But the height of his orneriness was when he bought a flock of cocks. He put them in nests on top of the wall, constructed at an angle so they would shit all over Neto's roses. Since Neto practiced organic gardening, more for economic than ecological reasons, his garden was full of thick, juicy, tasty worms. The cocks, in turn, swooped down to eat them and destroy the rose bushes. They crowed all night. This took Neto back to his old nightmare of cocks pecking out his eyes, his tongue and his crotch while bystanders mounted the triplets, who moaned in delight.

These nightmares were driving him crazy. In an attack of fury, he confessed all this to Ricardo Guatón, who advised him to concentrate his mind on other things, such as a hobby other than gardening.

-It's more than just a hobby. From when I was a young man, that's how I conquered women –I didn't have anything else to give them. You remember I was barefoot and I hid from the girls because of shame. But roses gave me the chance to buy my first pair of shoes.

-Look at the advantage of that, at least with all that fertilizer the drunks throw your way.

-It disgusts me to think about that. You know

how the economy and I don't like to think about wasting money on gifts. Today I have to, since it's la Merchita's birthday and I'm going to have to spend money on her. Gosh darnit in Heck!

-Don't pay any mind to all that. Look, tonight is presentation night at the Club XTC. It just occurred to me that you could recruit some people form the project to accompany you. I'll name myself first. The people accompanying you have to bring along a nice gift for you to pass on. That way, you save any expenses and la Merchita, instead of receiving one gift, get various.

-You're a genius!

-And since geniuses are always broke, I'm gonna ask you to not make me buy anything. I don't have any coin. Besides, I gave you the idea.

-Don't worry. For the others, it will be mandatory --A gift of a hundred dollars as a minimum, if they want to keep their jobs. If not, they can see how my boot feels up their ass. Tell them all that I know well how to apply the boot.

-I suggest that you begin with those who love to party. I'm referring to the platinum blondes in your crew, la Juli, la Morsa, la Brendona. I'd include her. It's about time you demand a loyalty test.

-You're a genius. You deserve a beer. I'll see you at the club at 8 P. M.

The news that, later on, that very night, they would have to pay out to buy a gift for Neto's mistress was like a bucket of cold water to them. The terrible group of the three P's: pendentious, *putas* and psychopaths, the Tecolote's trusty team went with nerves on edge, seated in a convertible belonging to Brenda, the most leprous and vulgar woman in the entire history of ESTAFASA, who thanks to her chameleonic talent, had managed to ingratiate herself into high society *soirées*. The head of Human Resources held her in high esteem and María del Carmen Martínez Morán, great-granddaughter of the honored General himself, always said:

-Ooh, that Brenda, I've never met a more refined woman in all of ESTAFASA.

Imprisoned by their uncontainable fury, Juli Travi, Morsa, Brenda and Loyda didn't stop shitting on poor Merchita. Above all because they had to skip a party in the house of some pedagogical consultants that night in Sonsonate whom they planned to trash. The car coughed *rash, rash*, their mouths never ceased to throw *splash, splash*, at everyone they found on the sidewalk, and that why they were seated on top of their seats, defying gravity. The four unleashed themselves, possessed by shared sentiments. They wanted to destroy or kill.

Soon, they arrived at a highway full of curves, where Brenda didn't hesitate to put her foot down on the accelerator, with the aim of *tolshoking* and thrashing the *kishkas* against the entire ambulatory machinery, when *rash, rash, rash*, the four heartless women had to abandon their distructive dream on the main highway.

-If we can just barely make it thanks to travel money.

-So, what are we gonna do, Brenda?

-Go to the party. Here I have some containers to fill with something special. Let's go behind the trees to get fart drunk. We'll give out packaged farts to everyone.

-Good idea, I wrote something about that a while back: the fart as a communicative competency, and, later on, the fart as a metaphysical essence.

-You're soooh intelligent, Morsa. You're gonna go far.

-After I gave it to Neto to read, he accepted me as a member of the editorial team.

-Bitch, having known that, I would have have written about the diverse essences of the fart, or the power of the fart as an act of contrition. How boring this is? Wanna hear my concert, girls?

Brenda squatted down on the ground to amuse her friend with a creative symphony in which she demonstrated old man farts, drunken farts, nun farts, heretic farts, soldier farts, sergeant farts, dictator farts and she was goint to start up with Neto's farts when, in the distance, a poor drunk appeared, carrying some books in one hand and a bouquet of roses in the other.

-Looky there at who's coming.

-Abused, abused women, from here on, we're gonna get some rods to stand up tall.

-Ooh, how are we gonna stand tall with an old washed out perfesser?

-Today's pay day.

-For us, let's say. *Zhivali, druzhe kurve, bolsha jarashó.*

-*As stari* as you are, Juli, *moya druzha. Vid-*

ya this *knigi* that the *stari* has in his *ruka* –and the old man grabbed the book with even greater force.

-It's not mine. It's the city's. And the roses are for my wife.

-Stop *kriching, stari yebegovnoyedi.* Your *slovos* give me a pain in the *ukho.* Shut up or I'll *razrezo* your *yazika* with my *nozh.*

-Aha, so you're the director of the school in... You need a lesson, *moy brat* –I mean-, you're earned it.

The *devuchkas* tore the book apart and the roses into pieces of pieces, which they threw into the air in hopes of creating the first snowfall in Salvadoran history. But soon afterwards, they did the same thing to the old man. They checked his bags.

-Look how this *stari chelovek* has *malenka* coin in his *karmani*!

They took 300 dollars in salary he had received that very afternoon, fortunately he had spent the other 200 on beers and roses and whatnot. Brenda kept a rose in almost perfect condition as a souvenir. Later on, they robbed a liquor store in a fight almost to the death. They left the owner naked in every sense, given that they stole his clothes as well as his money. With those resources, they paid for a taxi back to San Salvador.

When they arrived at the club, Brenda gave a deep kiss to Juli.

-*Spasibo* for the *dobro* time, *devuchka.*

Neto felt deep excitation at witnessing such a spectacle and even felt like going out to a motel with them in downtown San Salvador, but he abstained because that night was to be a gift to poor Merchita. The generous bounty of his stinginess only permitted him to buy a ribbon. In the wee hours, Neto would put it on his pee-wee so Merchita could open it with her mouth.

To keep her job at ESTAFASA, Juli gave two bottles of liquor to Neto, assuring him it was a gift from everyone. Brenda went even further, she handed over the rose she had saved as a souvenir of the crime.

-Give it to your friend. All women love roses, even those without petals.

The Cockslayer in Action

Here's a man who lives a life of danger
Everywhere he goes he stays a stranger
With every move he makes
Another chance he takes
Odds are he won't live to see tomorrow

The Ventures

Faced with constant harassment from Otón, who justly desired vengeance, Neto swore revenge. He knew that Otón, his personal *Ira Deorum* was not a man he could fuck with directly. If he killed the cocks, Otón, his own *flagellum Dei*, would cut his head off, if not worse. He had to find a way that wouldn't leave a trace.

He spent time observing the poet from his window to discover a weak point. It was easy to spy on him because he spent all his time in the patio, drinking lemonade and reading boxes of books that arrived by mail. They were gifts from poets in solidarity from poets from Chile, Costa Rica y Guatemala. One fine day, through his binoculars, he discovered him reading Gabriel García Márquez's masterpiece, *Cien años de soledad*.

-And what if he stole those books? No, when they found out, the poets would just send more. That wasn't vengeance. And if he brazenly killed all the cocks? No, everyone knew he was a man who didn't waste time with words. And with all his experience as a guerrilla fighter. And if he told one of his ex-wives, the one that came to visit him every weekend, that he was a womanizer? Nope. That was for men who never sinned. Thank you very much for spreading the good words to all the babes. There had to be a way...

In feverish desperation, it occurred to him to challenge him to a cockfight. The loser would pay fifty dollars and a housecleaning. If Otón won, Neto would clean his house. If Neto won, Otón would clean his house, especially the garden that had been turned into the official shit house of the poets who celebrated their parties at the ex-guerrilla fighter's house.

To his surprise, Otón accepted his challenge without batting an eye. He was so confident. Neto was so sure of winning that he didn't waste time. Right away, Neto encharged Ricardo with finding a first rate fighting cock. He knew he was a connoisseur of this art because he came from a peasant family. His father, his uncles and other relatives taught him to grow crops, butcher cattle, milk cows, cut cheese, package boxes full of products and, above all, take care of yard birds, especially fighting cocks. In his zeal to keep on the Tecolote's good side, he went to his uncle's farm, who gave him his best specimen.

-Return him to me safe and sound. If not, you're gonna to have to pay off all the money I lent you.

Ricardo was so sure of his uncle's skill in raising that kind of animal. He couldn't lose.

The days of the fight, all the Bohemian poets in the whole country showed up, cocksure of destroying Neto's house after his defeat. While they waited, Otón offered them beers and novels by García Márquez so they could pass the time entertained. One of the poets present, who liked to write about *atol*, pupusas and other native dishes, couldn't contain his desire to proclaim:

Here we are all well disposed,
In good standing and fine repose
Waiting between drinks on the rocks
The fighting of furious cocks
A dispute among the avian throng,
Song, good cheer and merry song
And a glorious afternoon
Bequeathed by our ancestors so fine.
For some the best is cock in wine
For my son-in-law it is heaven sent
Because that asshole poet is so hellbent
Like so many who have come and passed
He must commit himself to the task
With his stomach empty
And his fate attempting.

Everyday we get on the bus
You and me and all of us,
The learned and the ignoramus.
Because those in the know will make a fuss.
El Salvador is nothing but a farm
The Fourteen Families laid down by force of arms
An eternal fatherland of slavery and harm.

Others are lost on paths dark and old
Others are much more bold
Early risers like the cock
They give themselves up steady as a rock
Without delay, with firm faith to bets
Whose cruel spurs bleed them dry with debts
Such is the revenge of the fighting cock.

And when the bloody fight began
The contest of two beasts at hand

With their sharpened lunging feet
With their dreams so plumed and sweet
They will glory in applause
They will fear the whip in their maws
And if a feathered foe should fall
Then both of them will have given their all
And all of you shall see yet
When this tourney ends our poet
Will collect all the dollars bet
And join us in our merriment.

Everyone applauded the poet and they were so fired up with his verses they failed to notice that the fight had begun. Immediately, cheerleaders began chanting in support of Otón's cock. No one had imagined that the visitor was so well trained in every class of trick his master had taught him, an expert in the art of cock-fighting. As Vicente Fernández's song goes, --the cock finished off his challenger in two kicks. Everyone present was wounded by the commotion. Everyone present threw García Márquez's novel on the ground and joined in a moment of silence. For the first time, they noted a face of indignation on Otón de la Vara, but the most surprising thing was when, in a fit of marquezian rage, he screamed to Tecolote:

-I hope that cock does your wife the favor!

Everyone present broke out laughing and didn't stop discussing whether the writers of the Boom re-created themselves within reality or whether they continued re-creating reality itself. They immediately had the answer in the form of Neto Tecolote's impetuous response:

-Get ready, because I'm going to kill you.

Even though they were all puffed off with

emotion when they heard the tecolotic and marquezian words, everyone could see that Neto was a coward. All night they invested cheers, boasts and poems to call him out. He played deaf. Because of that, each and every one of them felt the right to visit Neto's rose garden to free the accumulated filth from their guts. Never had a public shit house smelled as foul as that rose garden that, at the end of accounts, no one deigned to clean. They only took charge of cleaning the inside of the house, under the supervision and say so of Radha. They took care to leave everything spotless, especially the bedrooms. Neto couldn't imagine the consequences of this nefarious cleansing, especially that of the bedrooms. Lamentably, he only found out several months later, when it was too late.

Meanwhile, Neto continued imagining how to avenge himself. Winning the cockfight was not enough, above all because they laughed at him and kept on using his garden as their personal shitter, to avenge themselves. One day, while he was watching Channel 69 on cable, there appeared a documentary by the great Russian cinematographer Boris Govnoyede, *Sibirske Yebekurve*, subtitled in English as *Horny Sluts of Siberia*. A group of naked Russian women were throwing snowballs at one another as they discovered novel uses for icicles. Eureka, but where was he going to find snowballs in El Salvador and could he, all old and squalid, throw them with enough force to kill. He came up with a wonderful idea after watching *Secrets of Famous Serial Killers* on *The Discovery Channel*.

A Russian psychopath, Oleg Kurvavich, killed with an icicle. He launched it with a slingshot against his victims.

Neto began to think how he could adapt this miraculous technology to his technological and ecological realities. At home, he had a 357 magnum revolver, an AK-47, a Colt .45 semi-automatic pistol and an old shotgun that had belonged to his father. It was a rather insignificant arsenal by Salvadoran standards. He decided to use the shotgun. It would be too difficult to make ice bullets for the other arms.

That night, he went to Lamb of God Arms and Ammunition, a branch of Hermano Toby S.A., to buy a box of shells for a twelve gauge shotgun. That Sunday morning, while his wife, the triplets and the little boy were attending services at the Tabernáculo Bíblico Bautista Amigos de Israel/Embajada Cristiana en Jerusalén of the Reverend and Benefactor Son of the Fatherland Edgard López Bertrand, S.A., he avidly went to work. He gingerly opened every shell and took out the lead shot, which he left where the cocks could swallow it as digestive stones. The more lead they consumed, the slower and heavier they would be. After ingesting all the lead, all of Otón's cocks sat on the wall like porcelain birds.

The second step was to very carefully cover the gunpowder with hot wax and press it down, thereby sealing it aginst the rest of the shell. Then he ground ice in his blender until it reached the consistency of sand. He put the ice in a plastic bucket in the freezer, taking out a handful at a time. He packed the ice down in the shell. He rapidly placed the shell in the bottom of the freezer. He repeated the operation until he filled all the shells.

A little after waking up at four in the morning, he took care to check if all his neighbor's lights were out. Satisfied, he crept through the rain toward the wall where the cocks were sitting semi-immobile. He carried a small cooler packed with shotgun shells. He silently and meticulously placed a shell in the shotgun. He got as closer as possible to the biggest and most aggressive cock without provoking any noise. He got to within two meters from it and didn't dare go any closer. He remained paralyzed for a few seconds and then pulled the trigger, causing an enormous roar and a flash of light. For the first time in his life he felt the pleasure of killing another living being.

A few seonds later, he heard a roar from the other side of the wall.

-You buttfuck! If you killed any of my cocks, I'm going to beat the hell outta you!

Otón jumped out of bed, he ran out to the patio to check his pet. He found him dead but completely intact at the foot of the wall. There was no trace of what had killed him, not even a drop of blood. He let loose a scream heard all through the neighborhood.

-NOOOOOOOOOO! That asswipe is gonna pay, he's gonna pay! TECULEROOOO! I'm gonna bust your balls, dickhead, that is if you have any!

Neto didn't make a sound. He waited a half

hour after Otón turned out the lights again. Then, he tiptoed to the garage. He opened the gate, which he had lubricated with coconut oil so it wouldn't betray him with the least noise. He pushed the car without starting it to keep from waking his wrathful neighbor. He went back to shut the gate and returned to the car with glowing smile, satisfied that he was the smartest man in the annals of knavery, silently boasting to himself about that simpleton Otón. He put his hands of the door of his Yugo to slowly open it and felt the sudden tap of a finger upon his shoulder. He looked around to see what it was and received a tremendous punch in the nose, immediately followed by a fist to the gut. He fell to the ground. Among the blood and vomit, which together had the color, consistency and warmth of *atol shuco*, he could see it was Otón, who had waited all this time to get payback for the cock. Before Otón could give him a kick to the ribs, Neto's gut emitted a sudden roar as it exploded, leaving him basted in shit.

-Shitty dickweed, so you thought you could fuck me and run away like a dog.

-What are you talking about, Otón? I haven't done anything to you and now you assault me right in fron of my own house.

-Don't play dumb, you pathetic piece of shit. You killed my cock and now you're gonna buy me another to replace it.

-I haven't done any such thing. I left for work and you jumped me like a gangster.

-Stop acting like a faggot... Tell the truth like a man! What happened to my cock?

-How should I know? Did you take a good look at it?

-Yes.

-And was there any evidence of a knife, of bullets, of a beating with a stick?...

-Nothing, just a roar and bright light.

-So you tried to murder me for the hell of it?

-No, motherfucker, you owe me too much. I'm gonna keep on paying you in hard money until you pay me with interest for everything you've done... And now, what happened to my cock?

-Who knows, maybe it was lightning? It's that time of the year.

Otón gave him a look of insatiable hatred and went back to his house.

Neto had to change clothes, wipe the tears form his eyes and take another bath but he felt happy in spite of his pain. He carried the scar on his nose as a type of battlefield medal of honor. He saw it as the price of learning the satanic art of riling people up, of making trouble for others.

Draculita

Do you believe in love?
Do you believe in destiny?
True love may come only once
in a thousand lifetimes ...
I too have loved... they took her from me.
I prayed for her soul... I prayed for her peace.

Iced Earth

Neto's most frequent visitor was Isa-Bel-Quis Fellat, or "Chabelquis." In spite of being named for the Queen of Sheba, she was neither black nor beautiful. She was white with a rat face and dyed blond hair. She had a network of metal on her teeth, which produced an erotic sensation as it rubbed against the penis. Thanks to her prominent upper canine teeth, all capped in gold, as well as her suckatory abilities, behind her back everyone called her "Draculita."

She left for lunch by herself everyday but always returned in Neto's car, which had polarized windows. The truth be said, she really never had lunch, as we know it, but went out to perform other activities necessary for her job. In spite of her diet, she consumed more protein every day than any other woman would receive in a week. And that was thanks to Neto, her mentor *par excellence*. He saw her as his mare and and he wanted to ride her to glory. In his dreams, he was the cowboy hero and she was the damsel in distress waiting to be rescued. Although she surely believed that she owed her job to seed-sucking abilities, in truth she was so stupid that she represented no threat to anyone. Like a roll of toilet paper, all her colleagues wiped themselves with her, using her to feel superior.

As a member of the Iglesia Profética de Monte Sion, Chabelquis swore before the Almighty that she she would not break her code of moral righteousnes. And she followed the rules to the T.

1. God comes first: Chabelquis signed a contract authorizing the church to take her tithe directly from her paycheck. She spent every Saturday –the true day of the Lord, according to her pastor, in church. This was in spite of the fact that her colleagues worked Saturdays training teachers in the rural zones. But Neto was understanding with his favorite hens.

2. Honor your parents and respect the Divine Panoptic Patriarchy: She lived with her parents and her earnings maintained her parents and siblings. She fervently believed in the Patriarchy. She never denied her mouth to any man.

3. Do not kill: Chabelquis wouldn't kill a fly. She would, nevertheless, saw the floor out of under anyone.

4. Do not fornicate: Chabelquis never let any man enter the temple of her body. She swore that the first to deflower her would be her husband, whom she would marry in accordance to the Law of God and the Civil Code. In ESTAFASA, of course, many murmured that Juli Travi busted her cherry; but that didn't count, because technically, Juli Travi

is female. Sucking the old Tootsie Roll didn't count either, even if she did it twenty times a day.

5. Do not steal: The only thing Chabelquis ever stole was the money of the government and people of El Salvador, given that she received a salary without contributing anything. That was inevitable, for anyone who formed part of Neto's technically and automatically became a thief. To justify herself, she memorized Don Netiyo's hackneyed advice: thou shalt not steal –a line she would repeat every hour as a bewitching mantra so she could feel that she was the most honest person in ESTAFASA. Chabelquis learned this demagogy from her favorite mentor. She also religiously believed in private property.

6. Do not envy: Instead of envying the oligarchy, she dreamed of marrying a scion of the Fourteen Families. She believed that material wealth was a sign of God's favor. But, above all, she was a resigned woman. If life had given her the opportunity to get hitched to Neto, she would've done so.

When all was said and done, from the moment she developed her sucking-linguistic competencies, she stopped being a target of the famous platinum blondes. Neto's team of psychopaths would have skinned her alive. But after her affectionate alliance, they had no problems with her showing off with her boss's arm around her. They gave her warm hugs in meetings, in training sessions and in all the halls of ESTAFASA. But what a great snack for conversation she became when she returned from lunch, with a delicious milk moustache painted on her lips, all attached to Neto's arm.

7. Be patriotic: She was a proud member of the Alianza Republicana Nacionalista.

8. Believe in the power of the Word of the Lord: Every Saturday she pondered the prophecies of the Divine Prophetic Episcopal Pontifex Manuel de Urdemales, who told her she was destined to be the wife of an important man.

9. Dress decently and humbly: She wore long sleeves, a long skirt and a white rag on her head.

10. Do not imbibe liquor: In accordance with her pastor's declaration that the Bible was mistranslated, that Jesus did not imbibe wine because alcohol was the invention of Satan, she celebrated the transubstanciation with grape juice and Ritz crackers.

Two for One: Juli Travi

Along the highway that leads from the Departament of Cuscatlán to San Salvador, a car from
ESTAFASA took off every Thursday at incredible
speed, dangerously passing buses, microbuses
and private vehicles.

-Hurry up, man, hurry. Licenciado Neto is
waiting for me.

-Doña Julita, I'm doing everything I can.

-Move it, man, pedal to the metal, don Fermín, like a Formula One racer.

The one yelling was Juli Travi Cornejolio, a
great friend and servant of Neto Tecolote. Every
Thursday, she had to carry out a visceral and
secret mission for the boss. The first days, the
chauffeur on duty imagined that it was an ur-
gent meeting related to the educational project.
Later he realized it dealt with a male need that
could only be solved through intimacy. In any
case, his job was to shut up and obey. Some
years later, when the chauffeur had retired
from ESTAFASA, he confessed that something
strange happened every Thursday:

-Miss Juli done yoosta make stops at Miss
Sonia's place, a lady who had a chalet at a school
where ESTAFASA yoosta serve. She didn't even
let me sit down to enjoy a good breakfast. Miss
Sonia yoosta give her four live chicken hens,
the way the boss liked'em. Miss Sonia yoosta
to make strange gestures and kept on repeatin'
the word "with" and when she said "with" she'd

make signs and gestures like she was imitatin' somebody lightin' a match, like somebody dyin' at a hangin' or somebody all squatted up in the bathroom takin' a shit, y'see. What's this? I yoosta say. Could this be a haunt? If'n she done took a look at me, my skin would start a curlin'. And the other times, I'd done wore me a scapulary. One certain day, I couldn't stand the curiosity and I done went out to Miss Sonia's patio. I done hid myself behind a tree and I saw Miss Sonia rippin' the feathers offa live hen chickens, only around the neck she was asqueezin' their necks but not akillin'em. She just left'em half dazed. Then she done put a wire right there through'em. Then blood spurted out their necks, and she put some gas on a rag and put it on their necks. You'uns know how gas staunches the bloodflow. Then she took out the wire and put a straw into the wound itself. After that, she plucked feathers from around their asshole, picked up some chicken shit, and dabbed it on the bald parts. Finally, she done put'em in a purdy little box, with pinholes in it so the critters could breathe. I never did understand what the hell was goin' on. But there, I never once asked questions. Our bosses always told us: "Shut your trap, don't say nuthin. NUTHIN EVER LEAVES ESTAFASA!"

Don Fermín wasn't the only, or even the first, to be dazed and confused by that woman's ways. Indeed, when Juli Travi began working in the Organization, everyone took bets as to what kind of tranny she was –whether she was a man dressed as a woman or a woman dressed as man. All and none were correct because Juli Travi was a chimaera in the classical sense: a fully functioning hermaphrodite. When she found out about the bet, her face became livid. She went straight to Neto, whom she fully trusted for various reasons –as her boss, mentor, marshall and mafia crony over a number of years, to the Human Resources Office and to the Supreme Director of ESTAFASA, a shadowy man whose face no one had ever seen, but who was related to the Fourteen Families, several obscurantist groups and a generation of ex-dictators. At the end of the day, her handbag was stuffed full of bills. She let loose a series of guffaws that lasted until she deposited the money in the bank. You could laugh all you wanted at her, but if there was a way to make money, she would take advantage of it. In any case, she gave the eye to both sexes.

Juli Travi came from a noble lineage of *mafiosi*. Her father, don Ruggiero, was the capo of Caltagirone, Sicily and aspired to be *il capo di tutti i capi* when his rival don Luciano made him an offer he couldn't refuse. He took the next boat to America, not realizing that it wasn't going to New York, nor New Orleans, but to El Salvador. It was a banana boat carrying arms to General Maximiliano Hernández Martínez in payment for the products of the sweetest part of the Americas. After disembarking in Acajutla, he went to the Italian embassy and asked for a position. He reminded the Excellent Ambassador that he had armed the *le camincie nere and i squadristi* of Caltagirone during the historical march on Roma carried out by *Il Duce*. After verifying those details, he was named as the embassy's *Attaché Militaire*. He advised General Hernández Martínez as to the best ways to eliminate the reds, explaining to him that fundamentally, the reds suffered from an abnormal retention of fecal material, something easily cured through a generous application of castor oil. The General thanked him for sharing his knowledge of high technology but explained that he preferred more traditional means, since castor oil killed internal bugs and that it was a greater crime to kill a bug than a human be-ing –since a human would be reborn and a bug would die once and forever. He didn't want to put his mortal soul in jeopardy.

With the arrival of the Second World War, the Italian Embassy was closed because El Sal-vador was theoretically aligned with the Allies. The General, therefore, gave him a house on Avenida Roosevelt and don Ruggiero opened a photography studio. With so many executions, there was a great demand for photographic evidence documenting the war against subver-sion. At the same time, don Ruggiero advised the General how to keep his secret friendship with the Fascists and the Nazis by establishing a base for supplies and petrol for German sub-marines. Unfortunately, the US found out and the General had to go into exile.

Don Ruggiero then dedicated himself to pho-tography with heart and soul. He was a sleuth, a master in finding bloody accidents, gory mur-ders and all kinds of gruesome matieral for the newspapers. He also took pictures of women, which he clandestinely sold in brothels.

After a few years, don Ruggiero married the daughter of a coffee baron and had a daughter. But, since he couldn't have the son he wanted, he dressed her as a boy, taught her boy's games and took her to work. But he wouldn't let her work in his business, despite Juli's most fervent dream of being a photographic artist. Don Ruggiero thought such work was relegated to hairy chested males, not for women. Juli Travi, therefore, dedicated herself to teaching, or rather the embezzlement of funds from educational institutions.

Juli's master trick was to invite her male colleagues out to drink, flirt with them when they were shitfaced drunk, take them to the Gran Hotel Oasis del Amor in beautiful Cuscatancingo. There, she turned out the lights and made love like a woman. As soon as they were asleep, she raped them and took pictures with a digital camera. Since El Salvador is the most machista country in the Americas, none of these men would ever deny her anything for the rest of their lives. She let it be known that she kept the photos in the Banco Suizo-Guanaco in case anything ever happened to her.

Her greatest delight was taking advantage of women, especially young teachers. She waited until everyone else had gone. She pretended to be a trustworthy friend to gain their confidence. Then she pulled out a rag soaked in ether that she carried in a sealed jar, to leave them unconscious and then do the same thing she did to men.

If this abomination to the human race had a

generous and caring heart, she would have provided love to a great percentage of the planet,
since thanks to six ways of providing and receiving sexual pleasure, she served every possible sexual orientation. But what God provided
for creation, she used for destruction.

In spite of her crude, monstrous and almost
illiterate nature, her family connections in the
party and in government, as well as her deli-
ciously malevolent schemes won her a career
in education. When all was said and done, she
boasted about her notable service to the Fatherland. No one knew with certainty, but it was
rumored that in the 70's she lent her services to
obscurantist, clandestine groups that dressed
El Salvador in mourning. During those years,
she matriculated at the leftist Universidad Nacional, in spite of her ultra-rightwing beliefs
and her vocation of writing children's poems
with fascist content. It was weird. Her own father couldn't even explain why she decided to
mix with the reds she so heartfeltly detested.
There, she spent a long period without graduat-
ing or even making headway in her studies for
a bachelor's degree in psychology. She invested
most of her time on the track and field team.
She religiously ran track every afternoon, showing off her expensive clothes, specially made
and adequate to call attention to her feminine
attributes. She tarted herself up in every way
possible. Naïve students made a hubbub when
they saw a tall blond with enchanting green
eyes openly flirting with them. Evidently, they
forgot their training when she appeared before

them in sexy sports wear leaving uncovered a pronounced bust and thick, firm legs as resistant as those of a man. She was different from the others... For many, she was an unknown, other exclaimed:

-So much sensuality, elegance, distinguished bearing, whiteness and golden presence wrapped in an energetic, athletic and virile aspect, almost masculine at times.

-She's the woman of my dreams –others exclaimed.

-She doesn't look like a plastic doll, a living room trophy, but an eager, royal, wellbuilt woman, capable of helping us transport war material to Guazapa volcano.

She lived to flirt with them, invite them to parties, to innocent dates from time to time. The strange thing is that most of those who were with her disappeared. Some rumored that somehow, snitches had infilitrated the university sports teams. In a single year, nearly forty had fallen. The saddest case was that of Coqui, a kid involved with the urban commandos. They say they saw him running after Juli, trying to figure out what kind of knot she had tied up between her legs. In the back of her shorts, she had a type of tube or odd sort of wrapper that didn't look anything at all like a tampax or a kotex. The young man was just about to discover what it was when he heard a loud noise. Some men dressed as para-medics carried him out on a stretcher and put him in an ambulance. And nothing more was ever known about his whereabouts. When the number of disappearances increased, Juli decide to escape to Guatemala. When she returned, she was named director of the Acovit school. The party never forgot her.

-As long as I don't do anything wrong, the party is so generous with me that just for waving a flag they remember me. I hope one day they'll award me a political position.

And if she were more polished and less greedy, she would have remained as the director of the Acovit school, where, it was rumored, money disappeared as if it were the Bermuda Triangle. She also would have kept her professorate at the Universidad Maximiliano Hernández Martínez, the only place where they could more or less prove she had graduated because the university was closed. And she could have even have still been the supervisor for Departament of La Libertad, where she was famous for her constant demands and abuse of instructors, including the time when she forced a teacher recently graduated from the UCA to engage in indecencies during the first week of classes. Who would deny her a favor in exchange for keeping her happy?

Juli Travi had the habit of pronouncing final "s" with an unusual intensity. Wagging tongues said it was because she had so many cunt hairs in her mouth that it prevented her from pronouncing correctly. Others maintained that it came from excessive alcohol, which kept her tongue asleep. In the same way they bet on her sex, they now bet on the cause of her dense esses. At the end of day, they discovered that both sides were correct and so, Juli Trabi herself claimed the prize.

Neto didn't protect her for her beauty and sexual attraction. He needed her at his side. She did his dirty work and provided the help of her relatives. Neto, for his part, let her steal, ruin, harass or rape any colleague, be they male or female. She had helped him enormously while he rose though the ranks and, therefore, he believed he couldn't continue without her help.

At the Klondike school, she showed up at six in the morning. She knew that Teresita das Minas was alone, so beautiful and angelical was the young lady. She put aside a fourth of her salary to buy sweets, used clothes and supplies for the poor kids in her class. The purity of her soul radiated in her green eyes, as beautiful as emeralds. In Travi's mind, those eyes desired her. She decided, therefore, to do whatever was necessary to be alone with her. She sighed for Teresita every time she saw her on her motorcycle and decided that she must be trisexual (men, women and motorcycles). That morning Teresita almost died of fright when she saw her come in.

-Hi, sweetie. I came in because the door was unlocked.

-Hi, *licenciada*. What a surprise!

-And the director?

-She went out to buy some things.

-So, we're alone?

-Alone, *licenciada*.

Little by little Juli Travi drew nearer while Teresita stepped back toward the wall. Within a few seconds, she found herself overwhelmed by Juli's strong arms and there was no human power capable of defending her.

-I just want to give you some pedagogical counseling.

-Please, *licenciada*! Not now. Don't bother. I need to catch up on my work.

-I see you haven't written the wall of words. I'm going to write some words on your body.

-Please, *licenciada*! We're educators. We don't need a scandal.

-Well, I'm going to give you one if you say no. I'm well connected in politics. Ask any teacher, especially those that serve my party. Now, don't be a dumbass. I want you to write a few words...

-Yes, *licenciada*, yes.

-The same ones I'm going to dictate to you with my tongue.

-Yes, *licenciada*, yes.

She knocked her over in a single blow and proceded to do what she had come for. Poor Teresita didn't even dare scream. The director found her crying unconsolably. She swore revenge and, with that purpose, wrote to Señor Licenciado don Néstor Tecolote demanding justice. But when Neto Tecolote found out about Juli's newest adventure, she burst out laughing so hard he had to visit the clinic for a tranquilizer. He'd laughed so hard he got lockjaw.

In spite of her great successes in the field of devilry, every time she found a good position with lucrative possibilities, she screwed herself due to excessive ambition, for stealing more than necessary, for imtimidating and blackmailing too many people, for selling so many grades that people denounced her. To which she defended herself:

-Gossip. They're jealous of me. I've never liked working with people who gossip. I only work with genuine, authentic people.

She never learned to enjoy success. A thief never steals more than what people are disposed to lose –that was the Party's golden rule. Luckily, she had family to count on who enjoyed great influence ever since her father arrived from Sicily, fleeing a misunderstanding with his partners.

With all that, she didn't do bad for a big-mouthed gossip who only had a high school education and a falsified degree from the difunct Universidad Nicolás Ayala, whose former campus is now occupied by the Colegio Lazarillo de Tormes. Like Chabelquis, her talent was her mouth, but she used it to destroy others instead of providing pleasure to corrupt bosses. At the same time, that tongue could clean the shit right off any superior's pair of boots.

As a cheerleader for the Party, she knew she would never lack for work, so she didn't care what others said about her. The teachers in one department were ignored when they complained in writing about her constant abuse of power, her insults, her incessant campaigning for the Party, her scarce visits to schools and the fact that she took more *mordidas** than a cloud of mosquitos. Neto, with satanic laughter, threw the letters in the garbage can.

Julieta also laughed after a few beers at the

---

*Bribes

Club Las Vegas. She remembered her deeds at the Acovit school:

-Your son has failed.

-But *Licenciada* Travi, we're barely into July.

-All the teachers have signed that he has failed.

-Then, show me what they've written.

With no shame whatsoever, Julieta remembered that she opened the top three drawers of her desk –all stuffed with bills. What times those were! What a great life she led with so much thievery! And to imagine that money is so fickle, as fleeting as the almond flower. She could have so much more if certain families had not gotten in her way. Especially that heartless old man who dared interview the teachers and that way found out that the signatures in her support were false. On many occasions, she used falsified materials. But the most audacious was a baker from the opposite party who dared demand that she produce her accounting books and show them publicly. Poor old man: His noble sentiments failed before that woman's malice.

She never discovered until too late that her own janitor provided information about all the families in the neighborhood. The community couldn't judge her formally. There were only complaints, which is why there have remained rumors about that thief and how she mananged to escape a free vacation in the Ilopango incarceration center for women.

She knew it perfectly well, that's why she never denied any of the special favors the Tecolote asked of her. Among the gifts most appreciated by Neto were the strange chickens she brought him every Thursday.

-Hurry up, don Fermín, hurry up.

-But we're making good time, doña Juli, it's not even four o'clock yet.

-Hurry up before they die.

-Who?

-The chi... Ay, hurry up and drive, man, that's what you're paid for.

Like greased lightning, Juli Travi got out of the car to greet Neto who was waiting impatiently in the parking lot. He took her by the arm and led her to the far corner of the ESTA-FASA lot.

-You're in big trouble. I told you never to let'em die.

-Ay, excuse me, Neto. That man wouldn't hurry up and there was all that traffic in Soya-pango.

-Look, Juli, I don't put up with you because you're my hen, I mean mare, I mean lady, not because you're so professional in your fucking. I like you cause you stretch me out, you rattle me, you massage me with those hands –half he-man, half faggot. You have things no other woman has. And it's not because you have pull with the people in the party. The real reason I like you is because you're the only one who knows about my perverted thing for chickens. You're the only one who understands my emotion, my attraction for chickens. I love the way they agonize in my claws while I suck their blood as it bubbles forth. And the, I like to rip the meat off the bone to get myself a rise. And above all, I like that part you female layers and hens have in common: the arsehole. But not that fried or stewed bunghole the old ladies in the diners serve –but the dunghole itself, that last hole, full of caca, full of shit: Without any cover, the asshole full of shit. But you came here and brought me dead ones. Gosh hecky darn!

The chicken mob is extorting
For months they've screwing me
Cause they know I'm a delinquent
A nighttime assassin,
A demented psychopath,
Chickensucker
Arsehole, a thousand goofy chickens
I'm a being out of control,
Illborn tecolote,
Messenger of death.

Gimme gimme some chicken
Gimme gimme some chicken
Gimme the chicken
Gimme the chicken.

Because we aren't born where there's nowhere
to screw around
There's no reason to ask us why we're gonna steal
If the gringos throw millions at us
We're gonna grab'em. . . .
LONG LIVE THIS MOB OF MOTHERFUCKERS
Feel the power of ESTAFASA
As gangsters we pull straighter
Why are we working with these asshole teachers?
And even though we aren't with that decent folk
We keep warm with our big mouths and lies
They keep on eating misery
Poor old schools
We steal from the people.

The Black Sheep

Men were wont ones off shepe to fede,
Shepe now eate men on dowtfull dede.
This wollwysshe shepe, this rampyng beast,
Consumeth all thorow west and est.
The Blacke Shepe is a perylous beast

The Blacke Shepe is a Perylous Beast
English ballad, c. 1550

Rebeca Ewì Bard Godoy felt unsatisfied with her life. As a graduate of Columbia University in New York, everything was too easy. All the doors opened up automatically for her in her career. At the age of thirty, she became the head of the teaching department at the New York Museum of Culture. She remembered how much happier she was when she served as volunteer in the Peace Corps and later on as a coordinator of volunteers who taught literacy in Nicaragua. There, in those days, she sweated blood supervising the construction, methodology and plan for funding for a school in Ometepe. For every drop of sweat, the mosquitos sucked two drops of blood. But she felt the progress, the happiness when the school opened, the great parade and applause when the children arrived on foot the first day of classes. Some times she felt the need to escape a world determined only by money, and seek infinitely richer rewards. Without a doubt, her five years in Nicaragua were the happiest in her life.

She when she saw an announcement in the

London Economist, she felt an attack of nostalgia.

What would you do to save the life of a child?

We are SalvaVidas, the most important NGO in the area of providing aid to children. It enrages us to know that there are millions of children today that still lack access to health, schools, human rights and adequate protection. We are determined to grant these rights to all the children of the planet and offer more and more programs to effect positive change in the lives of millions of children. We have already bettered the lives of children in wealtheir countries decades ago. Now, it's our turn to eliminate hunger, malnutrition and preventable illness in the rest of the planet. Together, we can all give a brighter day to youth. That's why we ask you to apply for the following position:

International Coordinator
of Teaching Methodology
$40,000
San Salvador, El Salvador

You will be the supervisor of a team of pedagogical professionals located at ESTAFASA, the Salvadoran NGO with the greatest influence with the government. You will be responsable for delivering teaching materials, food and basic articles of personal hygiene to high risk schools in the Republic of El Salvador. You will train a team of local personnel in modern techniques of language teaching, literature, mathematics and basic science. You will instruct them how to share these new skills in a humanitarian fashion with ill-trained personnel in the field. You will prepare evaluation material with rubrics for measuring educational progress. You will teach local personnel how to administer these systems and how to demonstrate the program's success. At all times, you will be in contact with the advisors at the nation's G-8 embassies. Due to the delicate nature of this work, by no means will you carry out work outside of ESTAFASA nor will you comment on your work at ESTAFASA. As part of our generous compensation package, you will receive an apartment on the ESTAFASA campus. In this manner, your key role will be to provide technical aid to the country, ensure successful scholarships and carry out institutional investigation to strengthen the educational system and extend access for all, as well as our principle of integrating theory, aid and the programming of future programs.

You must have significant experience in the field of teaching methodology and evaluation in both practical and theoretical areas. You must speak, read, write and understand Spanish and English at a professional level. It is also necessary to have a successful record in fundraising, influencing important people and managerial experience. REF: SVESSS13666.

All applications are due: 2 November of this year. To apply, go online to www.SalvaVida.org.US/jobz .

The position requires a Master's, preferably in Political Science, International Development or a related field. You must have five years of experience, including technical and administrative knowledge of development projects of the G-8 Guided Democracy Program. Said experience will demonstrate the abiilty to work within and understand delicate structures and minimalist governments and to administer programs under complicated structures. Technical and administrative experience in Central America is an advantage. Basic skills in computing are a prerequisite.

Rebeca felt immense joy when she realized that she qualified in every sense. She had ten years of experience working in the educational field. At the museum, she wrote didactic texts in various areas of culture, not only on paper but also online, multimedia, audio and video.

Three months later, she received a call from *SalvaVidas* to set up an interview. At the end of the interview, they offered her the job. It was the happiest day in her life. Rebeca truly wished to effect positive changes in the lives of Central

Americans and from now on, she would.

Everytime she looked in the mirror, she received a memory that she represented *The New United States, the United States of Obama,* not Bush's. She was short, slim, with copper skin, dreadlocks and aquamarine eyes. Her grandfather, Seumas Aoisdán Bard was of Irish ancestry. He claimed his ancestors learned to play the harp with the great Cearbhalán. His grandmother Jemoja Asé was Yoruba, the daughter of a Nigerian *babalao*, who arrived to study anthropology at Barnard. Her father, Sean Osain Bard, was a musician and musicologist at The New School. Her mother, Josefina de las Mercedes Godoy Hernández was the daughter of progressive coffee planters from San José de la Majada, who had to take refuge in the United States after receiving a white hand painted on their front door.

Moving and preparation took three months. Just in case things didn't work out, she took a leave of six months with immediate right to return and a six-month notice in case she wanted to come back later.

Meanwhile, they advised the department heads at ESTAFASA, at the G-8 embassies and at SalvaVidas regional headquarters. Neto had a series of meetings at various embassies with their personnel and those of the aforementioned NGO, where they formulated a common strategy and they warned Neto that if anything, anything at all, happened to Rebeca, that he would feel it in his own flesh. The British Cultural Attaché stood up and said:

-As my Abakwá grandfather used to say:

"*Ekue uson obonekué, erubé embori mapá, eri-ero.*" That is, "A goat who breaks a drum pays with his own skin."

They all split their sides open laughing with that, and the meeting was adjourned.

Neto knew nothing about Rebeca, only that she was an American citizen with some strange lastnames. He met with his cronies, Leonel "Macho Man," Ricardo "Shit Hair" and Juan Víctor "The Arab" at *Club 69* to further discuss the situation while they drank a few *Pilseners*.

-Technically, the Gringa would have the same rank as me, but since she knows absolutely nothing about the organization, and even less about daily, local realities, everything will stay the same. We'll give her an assignment to investigate that has absolutely nothing to do with nothing.

-Excellent idea, Neto.

-That way, we can keep her completely in the dark 24/7.

-How do you suggest we begin?

-The best thing would be to have her copy all the information on the Group A schools –in the coastal departments. That way, she would begin by working with you, Machito.

-'*Cause I'm a macho, macho man* –Leonel sang-... Tell me, how is she?

-In what sense?

-In every sense... Is she a blondy or a fire bush? How's her tits, big and juicy? Does she have a nice cunt?

-She must be another Pamela Anderson.

-But don't you have any photos?

-Ain't it enough to know she's a Gringa? Them bitches were born to fuck. They're big, so she's gotta have have humongous tits. Take your vitamins, because if you don't, she's gonna leave you all worn out. That's what happened to all them Gringos. They look like they only have half a nut, but the gringas rob them of their energy till they don't wanna fuck anymore or get their wang-dang-doodle sucked twenty four hours a day.

-And I thought they were like that because they didn't have any balls.

-No way, man. Them sons o' bitches ain't like that because they're a bunch of pussies. What happens is that once you take them away from their women for a few months, they become psychopaths, worse than our own.

-There, Major Roberto wouldn't have amounted to much. Look what they did to the Germans in two world wars and the Japanese still run away with their tails between their legs everytime they see a Gringo.

-And what the hell happened in Vietnam? . . . They shat the royal turd there!

-You don't know what the fuck you're talking about, your Shit Hair has leaked into your brains.

-Vietnam was like el Mozote but 24 hours a day, pure massacre, full time. What happened was they ran out of people to kill and they got bored. The reds, sneaky motherfuckers that they are, evacuated everyone and the Gringos sat around with nothing else to do but to play with their dicks. And as soon as the Gringos left, the reds, who had left town, came back and declared victory. You see how just a while back, the Vietnamese received Mc Cain like a god. And he was a fucking war criminal who dropped tons of bombs on civilians.

-Arab... how do you know so much about Vietnam if you're just a shitty Turk?

-I was born in Palestine, they do the same thing to us there.

-Ain't they Israelis there?

-Different cock but the same man fucking us.

-Ain't them some strange lastnames for a Gringa: Bard Godoy? Could she be Hispanic?

-They're Irish lastnames. Don't you remember that weird-ass play they showed at the theater last year, *Waiting for Godoy*.

-But my wife's aunt is Godoy and she's from Chalate.

-And they're all blondies up there because of all the Irish who arrived in colonial days.

-Tomorrow, we'll go to the airport to pick her up. And all you scumbags I have to put up with everyday will meet her and if we're lucky, she'll ask us to take her to a motel where we'll make her accustomed to tropical life.

At the airport, D'Artagnan and his tree musketeers waited for *American Airlines* Flight 991 from Atlanta. Although they paged Rebeca to let her know they were waiting for her, they didn't carry any sign.

-I know a Gringa when I see one.

After picking up her luggage at the carrousel, Rebeca waited until everyone left except a group of four men. She approached the group and noticed that they were waiting for someone. She decided to introduce herself and find out if they were from ESTAFASA.

-Don't nobody leave! Maybe she got lost in the stores.

-But those stores are only for people leaving the country.

-Then she must be in customs explaining something.

-Excuse me, are you gentlemen from ESTA-FASA?

-We're looking for a Gringa... have you seen her?

-I'm Rebeca

-Nice to meet you... we're looking for a Gringa, a woman from the United States.

-I'm from the United States.

-Fine, now stop fucking with us. We're looking for a Gringa and if you don't leave us alone, we'll call the police and you'll see stars and stripes all over your ass.

-I'm Rebeca Ewi Bard Godoy from the United States.

- No way, we're looking for a Gringa.

-That's me.

-It can't be. You must be from Cuba, Brazil or Panama, or maybe from the Atlantic Coast of Nicaragua or Honduras.

But not all Gringas are White!

When they heard that, Neto and Leonel left the group and took a taxi so they could be at ESTAFASA before the others and to spread the word. They felt completely let down. They were hoping for a Marilyn Monroe, and this kid shows up –she wasn't at all ugly, but they were expecting a Jayne Mansfield, but they were expecting an Angelina Jolie, but they were expecting a Megan Fox and here comes a Third World woman, Black, pretty, professional, hard working, pleasant, caring, brave –when they were expecting a 100% USA *sex machine.*

Upon arriving at ESTAFASA, the first thing Rebeca did was to present Neto with the Masterworks Collection of Classical Music by *Deutsche Grammophon* that the cultural section had asked for –ten CDs that formed a musical history of Western Civilization. As a joke, following the suggestion of the regional head of *SalvaVidas,* she also presented don Neto with a copy of musical comedy, beginning with the Broadway production of *Super Chicken,* which she opened immediately to play in front of everyone:

When you find yourself in danger,
When you're threatened by a stranger,
When it looks like you will take a lickin', (cluck, cluck, cluck, cluck)
There is someone waiting who
Will hurry up and rescue you,
just call- for Super Chicken! (cluck, awk!)

Upon hearing such an odious song, Neto turned red with rage. He waited till the Gringa left and then smashed every single one of the CDs with a hammer. He then put all the pieces into a bag and stomped it with his feet. He passed the micro-pieces through his coffee grinder until they became sand.

The next day, the director of the cultural section arrived to look for his CDs.

-What CDs?

-There they are, on the bookshelf.

-Ahhhh... those. They arrived empty. Maybe the customs agents found them subversive.

- Ahhh, I understand...

But the cultural director didn't understand anything. He understood even less the following Friday when, as he was going out the door, he received an envelope with a thousand dollars and a warning not to come back to ESTAFASA under penalty of incarceration.

In honor of Rebeca, Neto organized a general orientation the next day in which he emphasized the need for silence and for loyalty toward leadership as the key points of serving the people and educating youth. He ended every paragraph with the slogan, "Everything in ESTAFASA stays in ESTAFASA," thereby producing a sterile atmosphere of paranoia and "who-gives-a-fuck-ism." Neto, who had never been afraid of anyone before, obviously succumbed to something this dark, svelte woman, so obviously good and inoffensive, had. Her mere presence caused him various nervous tics until he had to excuse himself and leave everything in the hands of "Shit Hair."

He had scarcely left the room when he heard a ruckus akin to a second grade class. La Morsa threw a spitball at Leonel. They all began to shout. Some of the men tried to feel up the secretaries and ran behind them when they tried to avoid their attentions. Finally, they cornered them and overpowered them.

Leonel pulled a knife on Juli Travi when she grabbed his cock.

-*Drugi*, lemme *vidyerte* your *bolsha shlaga kharashó*.

-*Vidyi* for yourself *ili* I'll open up your *kishkas* with my *britva*.

-*Nye* you *interesovat sladka devushka*? Let's go, *malchik*, let's go *lyublilub*.

-You *pyanitsa*? I'll give you *bolsha tolchok*.

Juli then began to chow down on his tootsie roll.

Neto, meanwhile, blew his goods in the bathroom. He rested a few minutes, brushed his teeth and returned to the salon. Upon entering, he noticed a group of secretaries sitting on the floor crying, some male colleagues as quiet as Cheshire cats, Leonel lost in space and Juli with a brand new milk moustache. Before Neto could shout out to the devil's own thirty thousand whores, a group of ugly secretaries who were happy and grateful made a proclamation:

-Neto, what a *jarashó* presentation Shit Hair made. He did a magnificent job and absolutely nothing happened. God bless that *malchik* for his kindness and generosity.

Rebeca, who remained overwhelmed before such a bizarre scene, asked la Morsa what had just happened.

-Like you Gringos say, "When's the cat's away, the mice will play." You don't think you're any different from us? It's human nature. When the boss isn't around, everything becomes pure anarchy. If we don't have a gun pointed at our heads, we don't work, we start robbing and raping. You just saw that!

-But, why were you speaking Russian?

-Ahh, those were some words they taught us during the Civil War, just in case the reds won. They had planned to rape all the women and send the bastard offspring to Siberia as payment for the billions of dollars they received from the Russians. They thought, that way, we could disguise ourselves as reds and escape the country. Those reds only think about raping and killing. Don't you know that they themselves killed Monsignor Óscar Romero to libel Major Roberto? That's how evil they are. And in your country, the Communist Democratic Party still believes that lie.

-I've heard something like that.

Rebeca returned to her apartament to rest and try to understand the day's event.

Neto convoked his inner circle to warn about the danger Rebeca posed.

-I have a brother who's a cop, he can rape her and make her disappear with no questions asked.

-No, anything happens to her and we're all in trouble. I can sniff it myself with my tecolotic sense, I swear it.

-Wouldn't it be better just to leave her alone, let her do her job for a few months. She's certainly gonna get bored quickly in such a small country.

-No way, man. She probably came here to find herself a man.

-Then, we have to boycott her. No one will break words with that bitch.

From then on, everyone avoided Rebeca as much as possible either due to their own ignorance or out of fear of Neto. They had her copying reports in Section A in order to use them in Section B where they were doing political work. But from lies, truth is born one day or another. She figured out that something was wrong but she couldn't put her finger on it. Neto created an almost total blackout. He ended every directive with the slogan, "everything that happens in ESTAFASA stays in ESTAFASA," something that reminded her of the Yoruba proverb: "*aya awé iayé aa fisí!,*" that is "What we know stays here."

But the treatment her colleagues doled out to her, as well as her lack of contact with the outside world, truly troubled her. To forget everything, she decorated her workspace as much as she could and dedicated a diary to the strange events.

On the wall behind her desk, Rebeca had a black and white poster with the enigmatic words *KLAATU BARADA NIKTO*. In the poster's background, a man in a metallic suit looked forward with contemplative eyes. One day, Travi scutinized it and quickly ran to Neto's office.

-Neto...

-What it it?... Whaddaya want?

-That woman is a communist activist!

-The Black girl... the so-called Gringa. That scrawny thing... a communist?... Don't fuck with me!... I'm hungover. I went to see Merchita's show... The Gringa?... You're saying she's a red?

-Yes, Neto... She's a dyed in the wool red! You gotta see it for yourself.

-See what?

-She's got a poster of Stalin in Russian and I think it says "Death to Christianity" or something like that. I remember that the students at the National University said they learned something like that in their Russian classes.

Neto walked over to the desk to see for himself what Juli Travi had just told him and he returned to his office. He didn't bother to tell her that the National University never offered Russian classes.

-Well...

-Well, what?

-Did you see it?

-It's a poster.

-It's a subversive poster. If Major Roberto were here, he'd get God's honest truth outta her in ten minutessss.

-I'm gonna talk to my contacts at the embassy. Meanwhile, keep your mouth shut. I don't want her to find out we're watching her... in case she really is a terrorist. That's what they call subversive today, terrorists. And now they're all Muslims. That poster could be in Arabic.

-No way, Neto. The Arabz write in chicken tracks, just like the Chinese. The only difference is that Arabz write backwardz while the Chinese paint pictures.

-With chicken feet?

- How else could you write that way?

Neto called the embassy. His handler, I mean

contact, I mean *liaison politique* suggested that he take a snapshot of the poster and fax it to him ASAP. He warned him that if it were in Chinese, she could be *Falun Gong*, a group of nefarious subversives who were trying to take over the world through hunger strikes. If it were in Arabic, then surely it was *al-Qa'ida*. Neto followed the instructions of Malcolm Shithead (pronounced Sha-theed), the chief of political affairs at the embassy, to the letter. Meanwhile, all the employees of ESTAFASA slowly paraded past the Gringa's poster. Juli Travi spilled the beans –telling her to shut up was telling a dog not to lick its ass. She was going to do it no matter what.

Dr. Shithead remained perplexed by the photo. It wasn't Russian or Chinese or any other language when he typed the expression into the computer. Yet the words were familiar. He sat down to ponder the problem and arrived at the following conclusion –surely the words were written in code, a code with complex algorithms. But it was late and he went to sleep. It was there, in his own bedroom that his wife had a similar poster with the same words –it was from *The Day the Earth Stood Still*; a classic sci-fi flic from the fifties. The next day, he phoned Neto:

-Neto, I deciphered it. It took me a whole night of hard work, but I did it. It's something innoucuous but I did it. I appreciate, however, your attention to detail.

-Yes, boss.

-Neto... continue your efforts to eradicate

the enemies of democracy.

The aforementioned Dr. Shithead returned to bed, convinced that Neto and his group of clowns, and those who thought like him, represented the true danger to the country, the region and the planet.

Rebeca, in turn, noticed all the paranoia at the institution, since every talk ended with the words: "What happens in ESTAFASA stays in ESTAFASA." She noticed that Neto observed everything, that he had a network of spies and there were hidden microphones everywhere. Evidently, Neto spent more money on security than on programs. Evidently, the organization had a hidden agenda that ran contrary to what it proclaimed. Evidently, the key to everything was in Section B. Rebeca wasn't interested in digging up dirt on ESTAFASA, but in a country where everything was so superficially calm and quiet, there were deep primordial currents that felt the need to come up to breath, to show the world that there was something there before the Gringos, that before Alvarado, there was something there. Rebeca just wanted to work six months, learn everything she could and return to the United States, nothing more, but perhaps her black sheep *nahual*, maybe her *tonal* –for she was born on a good day. But for every stupid mistake Neto made, he stepped ever closer to his own doom. For however much he wanted to sacrifice that black sheep, more light fell upon him, more ferocious was the black sheep, until it grew fangs.

One day, Neto decided to send her to visit

schools in Section B, in complete violation of the convention.

-Juli!

-Neto?

-You gotta help me. I've had it up to here with that Black-ass Gringa bitch.

-So, she's no Pamela Anderson?

-Stop fucking with me! I wantcha to lose her ASAP.

-But, how?... She's a Gringa... I can't kill her, Whaddaya want me to do?

-Whatever it takes to convince her to leave.

-But, what has she done?

-Until now... nuthin... but my tecolotic sense tells me that she's gonna rat our asses out at the embassy. And that will mean the end of the project.

-But... if we just do what she asks us?

-And how many times have I done told you that if anything we've done reached the light of day, then we're fucked... We're the Gringos' garbagemen. They're afraid to get their hands dirty. Any piece of paper, any bit of information... and they bury us.

-So?

-Take her out into the field. Scare the living shit out of her... But indirectly. Don't threaten her yourself... You have to be the heroine in all of this.

Juli took her to La Palma the next day in a piece of shit bus, noisy with blasts of smoke, without brakes or shocks –and a fearless driver. Rebeca marveled at all the natural beauty in a country that, according what people said, was completely lacking in trees. There, in the distance was El Poy. They got off before the city and went to a hut where Juli bought two styrofoam cups of a coffee-looking liquid, dipped out of a plastic bucket and two pieces of dough in banana leaves plucked from the hot coals. She squeezed a shot of hot sauce into the cups. She handed a cup and a piece of dough to Rebeca, who received them with a grateful smile.

-Ay Juli, that's so sweet of you!... This is such a delicacy!... What's it called?

-*Atol shuco* and *rigua*. The *atol shuco* works miracles and cures everything. Where we're going now, we need strength. We have a three-hour walk.

Rebeca gave Juli a hug for sharing her food and culture. Juli, for her part, remained puzzled, she didn't know whether the Gringa was too stupid or too smart. Juli led her down a watery path between the cornfields. Rebeca was all eyes, checking out everything in detail, breathing in the country air, when all of a sudden, she heard a strong hissing, "hhhhsssshhhhsssshhhh." She looked above and on the branches of a mango tree there was a margay, a little tiger cat. Rebeca whipped out her cel and took photos while Juli turned white with fear.

An hour later, they arrived at a hamlet of bamboo and *tihuilote* branch huts, covered in plastic. The blue and white school was the only permanent looking structure. There was, however, a gash in the wall. The huts looked as if they couldn't withstand the rainy season. The director and the teacher waited on foot to receive them. They explained that the bathrooms didn't work because of a water shortage. The director sent a little girl to buy two liters of soda. Rebeca pulled out a twenty dollar bill and asked her:

-Is this enough to buy something for all the kids?

-Too much, we have two hundred kids but this time of year, because of the harvest, only a hundred show up.

-Is there a store near here?

-Of course there is... we're just two hundred meters from the highway.

Hearing that, Rebeca smiled to herself. She was very sure that Juli Travi was not the kind of woman to traipse through the jungles and the fields; it was all part of a plan for God knows what purpose. She thought about how scared she was of a harmless little tiger cat, and she smiled. She pondered the situation and she smiled. Only when the little girl returned with bags of candy and chips did she become sad seeing the misery of those poor malnourished kids. The little girl gave her a receipt with the change, exact to the penny. Rebeca put the money in the director's hands:

-Ms Director, would it be possible to use this money to buy a bit of meat and ask the children to each bring a vegetable tomorrow, even if it's just a grain of rice?

Seeing that burned Juli Travi up inside, bile was about to come out her ears, she was royally pissed with the smoke of thirty thousand demons. What she just saw was the strangest thing imaginable –to offer to the poor instead of taking something from them, to offer her hand instead of slapping them with it, to tell them sweet words instead of filthy insults. What kind of country did that woman come from to think like that? So naïve, so ingenuous, so goofy! Only a Gringa! Only a Gringa would steal from the legitimate owners of the country to later give to the poor –thus violating Jonah's Law: "if they're fucked, fuck'em more! Only a Gringa would dictate to a sovereign and independent country and at the same time demand rights for the homeless –thus violating the Funnel Law: Wide for some, narrow for y'all. Only a Gringa would deny the possibilities of free trade and then send food for all –this violating the Whale Law: He who takes, gets it all. That Gringa almost overthrew the fundamental tenets of Salvadoran society. More than anything else, she lost her chance to extort a chicken from the director. Of course, she would claim two on her next visit but now she was reduced to eating pupusas instead of the chicken she had dreamed of all day.

Upon leaving the hamlet, Juli Travi didn't even take the long road. She walked directly to the highway, took the shitty old bus just to Chalate junction, where she waited for the super-especial. She didn't break a word with the Gringa, probably because her mouth was completely contorted into a pussy face.

The next day, it was Morsúbela's turn to escort her. She decided to take her to La Coruña de Soyapango. In accordance to instructions, Rebeca took the microbus downtown, where she met with la Morsa at Parque Barrios at ten o'clock. It was like being at Coney Island. Rebeca arrived a couple of hours early to visit the Cathedral, Monsignor Romero's tomb in the grotto, the Palacio Nacional, the pirated DVDs on Calle Arce and the Mercado Ex-Cuartel. She didn't buy much and didn't carry much money, thereby using her common sense.

When la Morsúbela saw her, she bit her tongue with rage because she thought she would scare her by taking her around downtown, but Rebeca was ecstatic to see there were true artesans in the country and there were places to buy cheap clothes and souvenirs. La Morsa led her to the bus stop and there they waited for the microbus to Soyapango.

In El Salvador, the microbus drivers are a breed apart. Completely heartless, they are divorced from the human race. They are, rather, refuges from Xibalbá, the Mayan Hell. They are poor bastards rejected by the death squads for being too sadistic and marginalized by the gangs due to their innate cruelty, thrown out of mental asylums for being incurable, and so, they formed their own society. They see life like small children in front of a video game screen, with controls in hand. They earned points for being the first to arrive, for packing their microbus, pushing everyone, with arms, legs and heads outside, ever ready for the guillotine of traffic. There were always two racing from point to point, with amphetamine eyes, skin never bathed. They were a race of zombies who never slept. They were condemned by a cruel and terrible God to be chained to the steering wheel for the rest of their days of days, until Judgement Day. No one ever saw them eat or drink, they only shouted obscenities to the four winds as if it were their only sustenance. They were, however, magnets for single women, for desperate women, for the horny ones who could not be satisfied by any other man, for old women, for young women, for rich women, for untouchable women, even for nuns. Every one of them produced a wholesale chain of illborn bastards whose lineage went all the way back to Cain. But no one knew when, nor where these prisoners of perdition coupled with said women. Perhaps in the wee hours when they were chained inside their microbuses, women arrived in search of their infernal satisfaction. No chaste or Catholic woman, in any case, ever went anywhere near a microbus. They say that women sensed their microminibusic pheromones at a hundred meters. Even Rebeca, when she traveled by microbus, felt a tremendous urge to rub herself between her legs and had to withdraw her hand when she realized she was entering her erogenous zone. The worst was when earthquakes struck, when people went out into the street to sleep for fear of dying as their houses collaspsed into rubble. The microbus drivers had to find somewhere to park on the street and even though they were chained to their vehicles, they represented a great danger to the nation's morality and decency, given that once captivated by the pheromones, many women sleep-walked or crawled along the road of sin.

Others saved themselves, discovering at dawn that were at the end of an infernal line. And the music they played all day, the most shocking, the most vulgar, the most obscene, the most tacky –be it rap, ranchera, reggaetón or heavy metal; they sounded like the clarion call of the hosts of the Apocalipse.

But for Rebeca, it was all a great show: she counted how many poor suffering souls could fit, and her personal record was fiftytwo in a single microbus. She bought one of each product sold by traveling vendors who entered the buses, she always gave a quarter to every beggar –even those who didn't look like gangsters; she scrutinized the slums with a critical eye to calculate how many lived in each ravine. The two-hour ten-mile trip to Soya was a complete lesson in sociology. She ate a couple of pupusas swimming in fat –grease the *pupuseras* collected from the bins behind *KFC*, *Pollo Campero*, *Burger King* and *Pizza Hut*, half rancid but full of flavor. For many, it was a fun game figuring out where the grease came from –if that odd flavor came from potatoes, chicken or Italian spices.

They got off at La Coruña and walked a half block to a cement house. La Morsúbela knocked on the door and screamed her lungs out, "It's la Morsaaaaaaaa!" All of a sudden, somebody open a half dozen locks and the door opened slowly, a pair of eyes scrutinized the two women while from the back Paquita la del Barrio sang louder with every step until they reached a couch where a man was sitting, dressed in shorts sporting an uncountable number of tattoos:

Filthy rat
Scavenging animal
Scum of life
Ill formed deformity
...
Two-legged rat
I'm talking to you
Cause you're a scavenging varmint

Although it's the most cursed
Compared to you
It's still very small

When the song was over, la Morsa presented him to Rebeca.

-Rebeca, this is el Alacrán, some folks call him *Kúlut*, his name in Nawat.

-It's a pleasure.

-Likewise.

-El Alacrán is our guide here in La Coruña. If it weren't for him, we wouldn't have a program here and the children wouldn't have anyone supervising their educational process. And withour assessment or evaluation, the teachers would be lost, the community would have to shut the schools and very soon, we'd be like Cuba, where they don't have schools or food or clothes. That's why I give thanks to the United States for showing us the road to freedom and prosperity. If we were only intelligent enough to speak English, this would be a civilized country. We have highways, malls, five star hotels, American restaurants like Wendy's, and an army that's fighting in Iraq. The only thing lacking here is a civilized language.

-And what do you think, don Alacrán?

-Just call me "Alacrán."

-You speak English, what a surprise!

-I was born in LA. My brother wanted to go to college but he was born here so we switched IDs, so he could get financial aid. I got busted for gang-banging and they sent me back on the next plane out. I hooked up with some of my boys I met on the plane and here I am in lovely La Coruña, eatin' shit for a livin'.

-And your brother?

-He's fine. He made it into med school, damned motherfucker that he is. At least something good came out of the family. Being born in the USA didn't do jack for me.

-But things don't look so bad.

-You're right, here with a few bucks you can live more or less like in the hood in LA. But the things you see, the things you have to do for a living. That's not life.

-Then, what would you change?

-Everything. I'd make people understand, make'em work together to better themselves. Like my favorite song says:

We are the world
We are the children
We are the ones who make a brighter day
So let's start giving
There's a choice we're making
We're saving our own lives
It's true we'll make a better day
Just you and me

-And can that be done here, in this country?

-No, not unless there are enormous changes.

-For example?

-First, we gotta have governments in both countries that understand things. And the people here need to invest in the people here. If they want social peace, they gotta pay –that's why we charge rent. You can't live like a millionaire if the rest of the country is starving to death.

At that very moment, la Morsúbela, more furious than she had ever been in her thirty nine years, decided to change the conversation.

-It's time to visit the school. Don't forget, Rebeca, that we're here to serve the people, like el Alacrán said, we all have to carry out our duty. If not, the little will vanish like dust.

While Rebeca hugged Alacrán goodbye, in the corner of her eye she saw la Morsa pull an envelope from her bag, which she left on the table. If the money was rent or just a gift just to scare her, Rebeca never found out.

They left Alacrán's place and walked to the school. There, Rebeca acted dumb, she just nodded with her head when people greeted her. While la Morsúbela left with the director, Rebeca remained seated outside the office.

She moved the chair closer to the office window to hear the conversation between the two women.

-There it is, Licenciada, a plastic wrapped chicken, just the way you like it.

La Morsa explained that there was a change of plans that day, . . . it would be better to invite the Gringa to make peace with her.

-Could you bring it to us with two plates,

silverware, *picante** and lime? . . .

The director nodded. La Morsa opened the door and shouted out:

-Rebeca, you eat chicken, right?

-Not today, thanks.

It made Rebeca sick to think of taking food from others. Especially when a lard ass like La Morsa stole it from a poor woman.

They returned to ESTAFASA without breaking single word.

Rebeca went out with a different person every day of the week. It was all the same.

The Arab took her to a restaurant near Ilobasco junction. Then he took her out to the patio to take a siesta in a hammock, but that woman was nothing like la Loyda.

Shit Hair took her to the Zona Rosa to have lunch in a pool hall. Rebeca played 21 with him, without saying jack.

Leonel Menchaca, the most disgusting of the crew, took her to have breakfast in the restaurant of the Posada Auto-Amor, a new type of love shack for the monied class. Rebeca only opened her mouth to ask for and eat pancakes.

At the end of the week, Neto had a gut feeling that it was only a question of time till the Thirteen of Cocks would come... the Tecolote had sung.

---

* Hot sauce

The Arab

Well I'm the sheikh of Araby,
your love belongs to me.
Well at night where you're asleep,
into your tent I'll creep.
The stars that shine above
will light our way to love.
You rule this world with me,
I'm the sheikh of Araby.

Harry Beasley Smith, Ted Snder
& Francis Wheeler

Yahya Mansur 'abd-al-Kuss was born and raised in Palestine. He knew very well what it was like to eat shit tossed down from those above. He never spent a single day in his childhood without witnessing an arrogant act of harassment from the Israelis. After years of hard work on his part and harsh sacrifices by his family, he received various degrees in engineering and chemistry so he could work in the service of the future Palestinian State he had always dreamed of. His graduation day with a doctorate in Chemical Engineering was going to be his day of triumph, but he was arrested by the Israelis for "possessing knowledge contrary to the well being of the State of Israel." He spent eighteen months in prison because no Arab country would receive him for fear of incurring a possible Israeli attack for harboring a suspected terrorist.

Finally, a distant cousin who had gone to fight the Russian infidels in Afghanistan arranged a temporary visa and there he went. Unfortunately, he didn't know a single word of

Pathan or Farsi. He was also sickened by all the fanaticism he found all over. In the Israeli jails, he spent his time reading classic books in English or textbooks for other foreign languages but here, the only book permitted was the *Qur'an*. He was forced to witness executions in the former soccer field: couples buried to their necks and stoned to death for committing the crime of love, widows murdered for begging in the street, the poor mutiliated for quelling their hunger with a stolen piece of bread.

One day, disgusted with living off the crumbs of obsessed lunatics, he decided to walk to Peshawar, in Pakistan. In Peshawar, he learned enough Urdu to find a job as a teacher of Arab and English. After a few months, he'd saved enough money to take the bus to Karachi, where he found work as a naval engineer. He sailed the seven seas and the ocean blue.

Unfortunately, he didn't see anything of the world because the ship was always about to sink and he spent all his time fixing the engines –the owners didn't spend anything on their goose that laid the golden egg and now it was dying. He also didn't receive his pay. Desperate, he jumped ship in Colon, Panama to seek fame and fortune.

In Panama they arrested him as an undocumented alien. Since he didn't have any documents, they didn't know where to send him, although some suggested they throw him into the canal to avoid problems. But they were afraid he might be a member of a terrorist group and they didn't want the country to have to pay the consequences. They were sure he came from a foreign vessel, but since he played dumb, without opening his mouth, they couldn't return him to any vessel. The police didn't know what to do with him. So there he was, in the slammer, reading books in Spanish, learning the language little by little, eating rice and beans but he got along well with everyone. Since he had the face of a scoundrel, they guessed that he was probably a policeman in his own country.

After two weeks, they called the police captain.

-We've never seen a case like this, he doesn't wanna give us any indication of where he's from. He looks like a refugee.

-Then, he must be Nicaraguan or Salvadoran.

-But, Cappy, he doesn't even speak a word of... He looks more like a Turk or an Indian.

-No way, man, he's too black to be a Turk, too curly to be an Indian. And if he were a Black from here, he'd be screaming bloody murder.

-But, Cappy, how did you come up with that conclusion?

-Easy, those are the only two countries where nobody wants to visit or go back to.

The captain looked the prisoner in the eye and firmly asked:

-Nicaragua or El Salvador?... Nicaragua or El Salvador?... Nicaragua or El Salvador?

He didn't catch the first word but he had heard that El Salvador was a country where some Palestinians had prospered, so he repeated:

-El Salvador, El Salvador!... El Salvador!

-Then what's your name?... what's your

name?

-Name, name... name.

He started thinking, he couldn't tell them his name was Yahya Mansur 'abd-al-Kuss. He did everything possible to invent a Hispanic name, but he didn't know any.

-Your name, what is it?

Seeing that the Captain was fixing to give him a beatdown, he dediced to translate his name into Spanish, eliminating 'abd-al "slave of":

-Name Juan Víctor Kuss, ahhh... Cuca.

-Juan Víctor what?

-Kuss, ahhh, Cuca.

The Captain scratched his head. No one could be named Cuca, or "Pussy." He thought that most likely, his police had given him a little too many lumps on the head and had left him truly fucked up. They could never imagine that really was his name, 'abd-al-Kuss "Pussy Slave," because one his great-grandfathers was the bastard child of a Slavic concubine who serviced The Sublime Porte, receiving with open arms and legs all the distinguished visitors of the Ottoman Emperor and Khalif 'abd-al-Majid, *al-Amir al-Mu'minin* –the Glorious Khalif and Commander of the Faithful.

-Cusuco?

Yahya Mansur, now Juan Víctor Cusuco (Armadiller) grabbed that name as if it had been his own all his life. He liked his new name. Besides, Saint-John Perse and Víctor Hugo were his favorite authors. That's why he decided to add the name of his favorite character from *Les Miserables* as his second lastname.

-Yes, name Juan Víctor Cusuco Javert.

The Captain spoke to the sergeant:

-Tomorrow, take him to the Ticabus Station. Explain that he's a Salvadoran, that he doesn't have papers or money, tell'em the Salvadoran Consulate will pay his ticket plus any expenses.

-Yes, Captain. You're a real genius. Nobody else could've discovered the origins of that boy.

-That's why I'm Captain.

The next day, when he got on the bus, they gave him a paper from the Salvadoran Consulate and a stern warning.

-You're going to El Salvador. If you get off anyplace else, they'll kill you... they'll kill you.

He pulled out his pistol to emphasize the point. Juan Víctor nodded with his head and added.

-Yes, El Salvador... El Salvador.

The voyage through Central America by bus is one of the most beautiful spectacles in the world, especially the climb up the Valle del General in Costa Rica and the passage along Colcibolca, the Lake of Nicaragua, where lies Ometepe, a magnificent island with twin volcanoes. Since there were wars in Nicaragua and El Salvador at that time, he had to spend the night shut into the baggage compartment under the bus in San José and locked in the baggage room in Managua. But he enjoyed himself immensely. Everybody on the bus talked to him, they told him their sufferings and he ate up every word. They all shared a bit of food with him and so, little by little, he acquired some elementary words in the language.

When they arrived in El Salvador, they found the customs post at Goascarán abandoned. It was the time of the guerrilla Final Offensive and the customs agents took refuge in Honduras, certain that the guerrilla fighters were going to win. The driver called the terminal in San Salvador and they warned him to take the coastal highway that passed through La Unión, Usulatán and La Paz to avoid problems. In every town, the driver made another call and adjusted the route in accordance with their information. They didn't arrive in San Salvador till six in the morning.

Since there was no one to pick him up, the driver said goodbye to him, pointing the way downtown with his finger. Juan Víctor walked a few blocks to Plaza Barrios. In the distance, smoke poured out of a skyscraper at the Governmental Compound. There was no one in the streets but in the background, he saw what he wanted to see, a large sign that said SIMAN, a sign of the Arab community. But when he approached, he noticed that the department store was completely closed. He kept on walking toward Parque Cuzcatlán and later on down the length of Avenida Roosevelt, reading the names of all the businesses.

Finally, just before the Salvador del Mundo, he found a name that he recognized, a gynecologist named Butros Butros ibn-Kalbah. Although he was Christian, not Muslim, Juan Víctor was sure he would receive him as a countryman. He rang the buzzer and waited for the doorman and explained:

-Butros Butros ibn-Kalbah!

The doorman, a bit perplexed, opened the door and led him to the elevator.

-Third floor, number 334.

He grasped the first word and got off on the third floor. He went to all the doors until he found the name he was looking for. He knocked on the door. No one answered but he kept on knocking until he heard a voice from inside.

-Who is it? What can I do for you?

-*Anta Butros Butros ibn-Kalbah?*

A slightly confused voice answered:

-Yes, ahhhh *'aywa... na'am. Ana Butros Butros ibn-Kalbah. ¿Wa man anta?*

-*Ana* Juan Víctor Cusuco Javert.

He had internalized his new name without stopping to think that he also had an Arab name.

-*Anta Juan Víctor Cusuco Gavert?... ¿Ta-tkal-am al-'arabiy?*

Juan Víctor could tell by the accent that he was a Copt, not a Palestinian, but a Christian Egyptian. He explained that he was a Palestinian, who hoped that, as someone like him who had also suffered discrimination in his own country, that he would receive him like a brother.

-*'Ay, ana a-tkalim al'arabiy... ana falastín. Ismi Yahya Mansur 'abd-al-Kuss.*

-*'Abd-al-Kuss!?... w-ALLAH!*

Butros Butros opened the door and gave him a big hug, trying not to laugh too much at his new friend's lastname. He made him some coffee and something to eat, explaining that he picked the worst possible day to arrive in San Salvador, that he was hiding out in his office because he couldn't go out in the street; that he could barely believe that Juan Víctor had arrived from the bus station completely unharmed. He had been trapped in his clinic, watching fires and explosions in the hills and around the Governmental Compound. From time to time, they heard blasts of bullets, but nothing happened to them, just hunger and thirst when the lights and the water went off. Butros explained the situation to him in great detail and the options that awaited them in either case, if ARENA or the Front won. When phone service came back on line, he called his friends in the Arab community to get him an ID card and to see if he had family in the country. Finally, they found a distant cousin at the Universidad Centroamericana, Father Jorge Abdalcos, S. J., who had kept the lastname, albeit in a Hispanic form. After the failure of the Final Offensive, he took him to UCA.

Father Abdalcos advised him to forget about being a chemical engineer. The United States provided all the bombs the country needed and the government would surely kill him to keep him out of Guerrilla hands. The Guerrilla fighters needed someone with his knowledge of explosives and how to perfect them. He suggested that the most prudent thing to do would be something completely inoffensive and useless such a language or literature teacher.

-Let me see your documents.

-Here they are.

-This ID looks so poorly made that it wouldn't even trick an illiterate. Let me get you a real one. I advise you, therefore, not to leave campus. Here, they're not like the Israelis, who beat you down and then give you a couple of years to meditate upon it. Here, they await you with a thousand ways of torturing you and then they rip you to pieces just for the fun of it... Ahh, good, your diplomas are in Arabic. I'll translate them myself and change that to a doctorate in World Literature. But meanwhile, you're going to have to read everything that passes for literature in these parts.

-Agreed.

The next day, Father Abdalcos came back with some bad news.

-Cristiani says the Israelis ID'ed you as a "terrorist." It's no big deal. You're going to get your ID but he wants you to do a "secret mission" for him before he'll give it to you.

Salvadoran troops took him by helicopter to the Cristiani plantation on the slopes of Chaparrastique volcano. The moustachioed old bald guy himself was waiting for him.

-It's no big deal, I need you to help me formulate some good fertilizer, something that will help me corner the market. My friends tell me that besides being a Doctor of Literature, that you also have excellent knowledge of chemistry.

-I'll do what I can, your Excellency. The soil here is similar to that of the West Bank, dry and hot. I think I can adapt what you have into something better designed for the ecological system.

After two weeks, his Excellency was very satisfied. He found him a position at ESTAFASA as an educational advisor, with a stipulation that he never leave San Salvador during the war. Indeed, during his first fifteen years there, they never sent him out to the departments. They had him busy examining texts until one day, Neto sent him out to Oriente to work under the supervision of Ricardo Shit Hair. The Arab got along well with everyone, except Neto, who perceived him as an annoyance and a rival.

Every time Juan Víctor came by his office, he played Ray Stevens's "Ahab the Arab" to piss him off, but he'd just start walking and dancing to the music.

-Get that Black guy outta here. I'm tired of seeing that black blood sausage.

They transferred him right away to evaluate rural schools. He had to sweat blood. To insure effective work, El Tecolote and Ricardo decided to give him a mentor, an expert in the field of induction. He needed a first class induction. After much thought, they decided that his mentor would be Loyda Tecolote George, a young lady, by the way, who just happened to be the granddaughter of Chón, Neto's mom's aunt. Loyda's mom was half Jamaican, from the Bay Islands. Inspite of her black skin and acid personality, Neto put up with her because she was his niece. In reality, she was the only blood relative he had in the whole world, or could admit to, at least. She also spoke English, thanks to her mother and she translated all the documents from the United States for Neto, who assured everybody that he read English. In ESTAFASA, that family relationship was a secret. He managed it well. Only a few really knew about it. As Neto's relative, she was free to do whatever the hell she felt like, and whatever she did made her feel good.

It's not like Loyda was a whore, she just did it with everyone for pure pleasure. And if it was sexual, her tastes knew no limits. Her own uncle had taught her to love love without any attachments. Without any more appreciation than it "lives within me," as expounded by the illustrious Alberto Masferrer, the greatest brain in Salvadoran history, according to the country's lesser brains.

No man ever slept with Loyda for her beauty, but for her dedication to fucking. She made a symphony of fanfares, sonatas and cantatas, a zoo of roars, screeches and moans, a cryptological conspiracy of whispers, mumbles and dead words chopped to pieces and a tesserae of dozens of living and dead languages.

Her orgasms became ever more musical until the Arab could not live without her music of the spheres, because there, in his promised land, he had found his own Scheherazade.

To tell the truth, the verbo-linguistic functions of her poetry could only be equaled by the last chapter of *Altazor* and the third book of *Finnegan's Wake*.

This devotee of fornication contorted herself into images only seen in the books of the *Kama Sutra*, only seen in the temples of Tamil Nadu, only imagined in a mind as fertile as that of the grand philosopher of porno, Larry Flint. For every syllable she expressed, she had dozens of movements. Only Loyda could turn love into dance, into *capoeira*, into one of the fine arts, into a discipline, into a religion.

And Juan Víctor was her pupil. He never found, among his lovers in the Orient, a woman so daring, so expert, so magisterial. And if such a woman had existed, she would have been *haram* in every sense –she would have either ended up beind the bars of a *harem* or in a pit ready to be stoned to death. But Loyda, thanks to her sexual magistry, was more monumental than *al-Ahram*, the Egyptian pyramids, prohibited by onomastics.

Loyda followed her uncle's recommendations to the T. On the other hand, as the generous woman she was, she offered Víctor lodging in the Armadiller Inn... room and board and a piece of quim. In regard to the induction, it was miraculous. In all the history of that type of labor assignment, no one had been so creative, diligent, engaged, passionate. That woman loved her job. But to pacify some critics opposed to this affirmation, let us exam in detail the lexical meaning of the word that serves to qualify Loyda's glorious task: Induction: Incitement or instigation to do something. Rational method that consists of reaching a principle that logically derives from particular facts or actions.

Víctor was injected with the new labor dynamic. He jumped head first into the flow of work, trying to fit into the accelerated, intense, maddening, pressured, sweaty and fatiguing rhythm that his mentor had set for him. She helped him develop the educational method in body and soul, until both found themselves synchronized in the same linguistic principle, derived from the necessary abilities to reach success in a communicative context determined by urgency, by hunger, by the beast of speed.

Morsúbela

Morsa Bisontina Amorfa was a flesh and blood
Maritornes –but only physically. She was as
sharp and evil as the Quixotic heroine was good
and simple. Although some tongues wagged
that her name used to be Marta in her obscure
and inelegant remote past, as she tried to make
believe in her constant fantastic discourses,
but that later she changed it to appear more elegant, in honor of the Countess Morsa Eufemia
del Condado de Bisonte y Cataluña. Although
others claim that name change was due to a
bad experience she had with a Mexican dandy
who despised her at the Chapultepec Zoo. She
wished to perpetuate that memory. Perhaps
because of this it was so difficult to follow the
trail. But she managed to become one of Neto's
favorites, inspite of not quite meeting the cri-
teria of the "Three S's:" "Sexy, Psychotic and
Suckup," but she was endowed with a deformed
poisonous tongue that only served to weave in-
trigue and falsehood. In her mouth, there was
no room for truth. She lied out of compulsion.
Sometimes, she told contradictory lies to the

same person four or five times in a single afternoon. But this didn't matter because, under the influence, she let it be known that she was Susana Gusana's sister-in-law, or rather, the cousin of Susanita's husband, the sister-in-law of one of her friends, of the boyfriend of the maid of the late General Maximiliano Hernández Martínez, and that she was also the lover of the former mayor of a small municipality in the glorious Department of La Libertad. And you'll say if you like to risk everything: check out her true identity, then you're not gonna have a job when you show up tomorrow. And if you don't check out her identity, at least la Morsa Amorfa is gonna have to dance that sweet *cumbia*.

La Morsa Amorfa was so proud of her collection of degrees: a Licenciatura in Business Administration from the UCA, a Professorate from the National University, she was going to do her Master's with visiting professors from the l'Universitat d'Alacant at the ESTAFASA campus. But that liar didn't have a degree from the UCA of even from her *cuca*. If you asked her if she knew Licenciado don Catrín de la Fachenda at the UCA, she'd say she didn't study there but at the Universidad Nacional. If you asked if she took a course with Doctor Ludwig von Drake at the Nacional, she would tell you she studied at the UCA.

Like Neto, la Morsa Amorfa had avian aspects. But she didn't have the form of a tecolote or an eagle, but rather the round form of a plucked headless chicken. She also had the breasts of a headless hen. But, since her cogodmother, Juli Travi, protected her, la Morsa Amorfa could say whatever hogwash that came to mind. No one ever saw the two macking, but everyone suspected it.

Inspite of not knowing the most rudimentary facts of education, they let her make an ass of herself in all the schools in Sonsonate to show everyone what a doofus she was. Her redeeming feature in Neto's eyes was her malicious tongue, which served to make false accusations against any employee she didn't like or who came between her and her plans of being the best, the group leader. One whopper she told was that she was Susana Gusana's sister-in-law. That was her secret weapon. But what that fool Susana didn't know was that Morsa was capable of anything to get ahead, like taking her husband away, or even, the best of her most gratifying deeds: poisoning the yogurt Susanita had for breakfast every day.

-Ay, Susanita, if I were you, I'd never eat anything that your dear sister-in-law prepares! Take care of yourself or you're gonna find worms in your rice.

Daring and nosy like no one else, one night shortly after beginning her job at ESTAFASA, taking advantage of the fact that in the auditorium of said place, they were presenting the walruses of the Circus *Animali Mutanti*, she let herself into Neto's office to find answers to her great questions:

-Why does a project funded in the millions not offer quality service for schools? Why are there contradictions in the budget? Why does a project of this nature hire so many jokers, like her? What was the true amount of money donated to the agency from that frozen country? How much money is being pocketed? Was her best friend, Julieta Travi, transporting political propaganda in ESTAFASA vehicles and embezzling the donations of that frozen country?

If she managed to find this out, she could blackmail Neto and her beloved sister-in-law Susana Gusana. But like a good tecolote, Neto scented danger. He left the show and ran to his office, where he found that perverse venomous creature nailed to his desk.

-Working late, ma'am?

-Ahh, you scared me. I was just putting these papers in order, these...

-Secret files? How did you open them?

-Well, I just typed in the name "Geraldo," that of your chihuahua. This is all very interesting.

Neto gave her a threatening glare, he made her step backwards toward the giant window while he nailed her with his furious tecolote stare. He noticed that la Morsa was not afraid. She made an effort to show that she was scared in order to apologize, to appease him. For the first time, he had found himself with a psychopath superior to his level. She did not feel emotions and perfectly manipulated human emotions. He was in danger. That woman was a true threat. At that moment, he remembered the other story related to her name –people rumored that her pathology was augmented during adolescence; due to a blow she received by a Mexican dandy. The poor boy experienced a terrible feeling of disgust when she was daring enough to steal her first kiss from him. As he tasted the bitter, rough nature of her amorphous tongue, he entered a state of shock and threw her into the walrus tank at the Chapultepec Zoo. From then on, she took the name of Morsa. She swore that one day she would return to Chapultepec.

-Neto, how can you be so cruel with someone so insignificant? I'm just a...

-Don't you know curiosity killed the cat?

-I'm not a cat, I'm a *gatúbela*, a catwoman... I mean... I'm a pedagogical assistant.

-These papers are my legacy. Nothing can break the code...

-Okay... Go ahead... Intimidate me... Kill me...

-Yes... maybe I will...

Morsa Amorfa saw him as determined. She saw a murderer's look on Neto's face. She realized that there was no escape because he had trapped her against the window glass. But the madman laughed his lungs out and her adrenaline stopped flowing, but, just in case, she prepared her secret weapon: her tongue.

-If I were you, I wouldn't joke like that, Neto. I have you figured out. I know you're stealing and I've already sent out some e-mails with scanned evidence to my Dad. If anything happens to me...

-Don't blow smoke up my ass! Your beloved sister-in-law knows everything. You'd better dance the mambo that I put on. But, speaking of secrets, I also know yours. I know you never studied at la UCA. That you're not a Bachelor in Business Administration, like you tell everybody. That you've never been a manager of any

Salvadoran bank in all your life. That your abuse of credit cards is the only thing that has kept you in a bank. That you've never been married in all your life. That your imaginary husband was never a top executive in any bank. That you also failed to study at the National University. That you only have a degree at la Gavidia as a teacher –and surely you bought it on the street. That you don't even have a pot to piss in. Want more? I also know that you have various suits against you for running over a teacher. Want more? I also know that you have another suit for embezzling funds at a school where you were a treasurer. But when you came to ESTAFASA you said it was a suit due to abandoning your post. They really miss you there.

-Ha ha ha. No doubt you're a snitch for the CIA.

- Yes. Lots of folks say I am the CIA.

-But you forget that I also know your little secrets.

Morsa pulled a torn piece of paper mended with Scotch tape. And she showed it to Neto in a state of maniacal trance. Between uncontainable guffaws, she revealed the truth to him.

-There's nothing that a little bit of patience and Scotch tape can fix. Here I have your original birth certificate and other documents, which show you are the bastard son of a *shuquera*.

-No... No, please. Mor... Morsa... Lady... Lady, please.

-Mmm and don't you bother taking them away from me because my lover, the former mayor, has copies of the mysterious birth certificate and other documents you had done away with.

Neto fell to his knees and in the midst of a weird tecolotic attack, he moved his gullet and his arms as if he wanted to fly, and at the same time, he pecked at the foul fishy smelling feet of la Morsa. Perhaps, for that reason, he didn't dare kiss them good. Neto was channeling a soap opera that no Mexican television station had ever turned its nose up at. Among his tecolote screeching he never ceased repeating:

-No... No, please. Mor... Morsa... Lady... Lady, please.

-You're a bastard. Did you hear me well? B-A-S-T-A-R-D.

Finally, Neto remembered he was dealing with an evil being of his same ilk. A cold-blooded psychopath even topped his genius. The more he suffered, the more la Morsa enjoyed herself.

With such a perfidious soul, he only had one alternative. Neto, in his role of despicable tecolote, had the stones to do it.

-Curiosity killed the cat.

-What?

Neto looked at her with the eyes of an infuriated tecolote. A malignant brilliance shone in his stare. But, once again, he broke out in guffaws, and la Morsa let her guard down.

-Ahh, for a moment I thought...

-Ha ha ha. I'm kidding you.

Neto ripped the papers out of her hand and with lightning speed, threw her through the window. In spite of her scream, no watchman drew near to the scene of the events. The noise of the circus was deafening. Mysteriously, some walruses escaped from their pools and wandered around all of ESTAFASA. On the grass, they found the corpse of la Morsa. They licked her blood, they mounted her, they applauded her, they licked her hands, her face; they tasted without disgust the bitter and poisonous taste of her amorphous tongue. That was her first real kiss. That was her first kiss that came from love. And, just as in the fairy tales, where princesses wake up when they are kissed by a prince, Morsa Amorfa refused to be left behind. The beast's saliva brought her back to life. Now, she would wander the world even stronger, more savage, more heartless, more demonic than ever. In her body there dwelled the untamable soul of a walrus. For once and for all time the nature of the hypothesis regarding her name was solved. From now on, she would be *Morsúbela*, the Walrus Woman, that is.

The night of the crime, Neto returned to the walrus show and later gave a ride to his night's companion, *la Merchita*, whom he had already dumped to give way for more space in his playboy agenda. "I don't know what to do with so many hens coming after me," he confessed from time to time with his crony Ricardo "Shit Hair" Guatón Basovia. And that dude, like any good suck-up, always had the right words to urge him on and make him believe he really was a *James Bond 007*. The night of the crime, he tried to make love to la Merchita, but a flock of phantasmagorical chickens assaulted his imagination, the echoes of cock-a-doodle-doo drummed so strongly in his ears that on various occasions his own cock-a-doodle-doo fell dead. The worst was that afternoon, he had announced with fireworks and circus fanfare the size of his joint:

-Get ready, Merchita cause today you're gonna meet a macho man.

Sick of waiting days and all of a sudden follow him to bed and nothing, she decided to whip out the knife her other boss, the manager of the show bar, had presented her for her excellent demonstrations of boxing. Full of rage, she screamed several times:

- Did you not tell me to get ready, then!

He got off on the wrong foot while arriving to Apopa when his miracle cream started working. It was an ointment that Ricardo "Shit Hair" Guatón had picked up for him at the Sagrado Corazón flea market, a place where he frequently shopped due to the sweet vendor women who buttered him up and invited him to a beer. What a tremendous situation. He had to park two blocks from his house and just after he finished his necessary, delicious and forced jerk-off, he noticed the presence of some gangstas from the Mara 18. The accelerator never failed him and so he was able to save his skin. But it didn't save him from asswhipping Radha dished out to him, when she smelled the foul stench in the back seats.

That night he couldn't sleep. The images of cocks assaulted his memory. The next morning, he found himself with a shelf full of books in his bed. All were copies of the novel *Mister President* by Miguel Ángel Asturias. Neto's tecolotic antennas lit up. Lit up with rage, he went to the closet and found another row of the same novel and a row of One *Hundred Years of Solitude* by Gabriel García Márquez. The worst part was that all the books had marker written in the same chapters: *Angel Face* and *The History of a Certain Prudencia Aguilar.* He didn't need to look any further. Ever since Radha began cheating on him, a strange series of fetishes appeared in the house. Every once and awhile, in the closet, there appeared every type of sexual fetish such as a rabbit's foot, fuzzy dice, four-leafed clovers, horseshoes, whips, men's underwear, a bull prick, panties, tombstone dust, black cat bone, dildos, handcuffs, rubber panties, a black leather cap, a barbed wire bracelet, a dog collar, a buttplug in the form of a screw, lollipops, a chicken head, a black cat skin, a shark tooth. The number of each object indicated how many times she had slept with the same guy. Neto refused to count the books. He only asked himself for hours on end who was reading such trash with her, when they began and when they ended the readings. He had no proof. It was only based on smells and other people's mumblings. As a psychologist, he knew perfectly well the typical behavior of a horny, unfaithful woman, but except for this, he had no proof. It was probably because he didn't care. It was probably because he also did his own thing. It was probably because it excited him to enter into competition with his wife's perversions. It was probably because he had only half a nut. It was probably because his cock-a-doodle-doo didn't rise up and crow like it used to do. This and other caviling formed in his mind as he contemplated his elk horns in the mirror.

The Literary Man

*El Señor Presidente de la República
quiere matar los piojos de los escritores
con puñaladas.*

Roque Dalton

He was sure he didn't love her, but that discovery had wounded his shabby unfeathered tecolote pride, and all day long at ESTAFASA he only moped:

-And with a literary man. At least, among my hens, I've had consumers, suck-ups, crybabies, maneaters, psychopaths, hermaphrodites, lepers, whores, all excellent in their professions, but never have I humiliated myself with an intellectual. But Radomira has no qualms against running around with a literary man. To Heck with that!... With a literary man. But I swear by my ancestors' feathers that I'm gonna find that pocket-sized dreamer.

When the clock struck five, he went over to Ricardo "Shit Hair" Guatón Basovia's office to ask for advice. The reek of *tamales pizques* with *chile* and *atol shuco* filled the air in that whole corner. Every afternoon, that glutton bought every kind of Salvadoran munchy from don Patricio, a street vendor. And since he was a pal of the boss, he gave himself the luxury of bringing in a folding table and a set of silverware that his devoted wife had prepared him. Neto almost bowled over from from the stench.

-And if the Head of Human Resources comes, whatcha gonna tell her?

He questioned him trying to contain himself. Shit Hair, because he knew too many secrets that would put Neto away, didn't worry about apologizing and he just limited himself to showing his mouth, full of *tamales pizques*, the kind covered in ash and filled with beans. But what almost caused him another attack of his strange malady, *Tecoloticus circuíticos amorfis*, was the novel *Cien Años de Soledad* that was on his desk.

-Is that piece of crap yours?

-No. It belongs to the Arab, your niece Loyda's husband.

-And where is that motherfucker?

-I got him working in Oriente, covering the schools in La Unión.

-Are you sure?

-Yes. He hasn't been out of that area for twenty days. Today he had to take a raft to Meanguera. He was well equipped with two pounds of pigskins from Jocoro. The kind he likes so much. I told him him not to go, to show up here at ESTAFASA. But he didn't pay me no mind.

Upon hearing that, poor plucked and tortured Neto began to control his niece on the cel phone. He wanted to be sure that the Arab wasn't responsible for his wife's new slip-ups.

-Fuck'em good he recommended her every fifteen minutes. Give'em your delicious ass. Don't let'em get away.

Loyda never figured out what she owed so

much harassment to, but since she needed to keep her job, she kept hcr trap shut, all screwed up and quiet, until one day el Tecolote told her to fuck her obsessions.

Since he was almost never at home, he almost forgot he had a neighbor, a certain archenemy, Otón de la Vara. One of the triplets told him about a handsome man, with long hair, a seductive look, a true gentleman whose business was cockfighting. That revelation drove him crazy. He felt worried about the marked enthusiasm his daughter showed for his scoundrel neighbor. She told him about that hairy seductor with so much enthusiasm. But he didn't pay attention because at that moment he discovered that the bathroom plumbing was broken and he had to use a pit latrine, which had been abandoned long ago. He carried a bunch of rolls of toilet paper, but he kept it in the bag because in the distance he heard his party's popular and bloody anthem. The music came from a pickup that visited neighborhoods in the Apopa area to hand out pamphlets, banners, caps and all kind of propaganda materials. Like a good citizen, Neto ran to the house, pulled out the photo of Major Roberto he kept in his drawer and placed it on the altar, next to the clay dolls he inherited from his mother and entusiastically sang his party's inglorious anthem.

When he was finished, he answered nature's call. He spent a long time dreaming of new projects that he would win as soon as his candidate occupied the presidential throne.

-By then, I'll be even stronger.

Saying that, he reached out his hand for the toilet paper. At that moment, he noticed that it had disappeared.

-That's weird. I brought ten rolls because a bunch of chickens shat on me. And the toilet always overflows.

He couldn't call anyone because he was several meters from the house, almost next to his new neighbor's property line. Suddenly, through the old piece of plastic, all full of holes, that served as a window, he spied the silhouette of a man with long hair who was carrying several bags of ice.

-I'm your favorite neighbor. I was talking to your wife and your beautiful daughters. Since I'm new, I don't have much stuff at my house, so I grabbed the toilet paper. My favorite slogan is "Take whatever you can and more from your neighbor..." But on the corner, a pickup handed me these posters and pamphlets. It's good paper, I use it myself in these situations.

-And so, what's your name? I can't see, but your voice sounds familiar.

-I'm Otón de la Vara, your favorite neighbor. Although your wife likes to call me Oto, Otito, and even Ceroto. But she does it with affection. Ah... by the way, I'm gonna make some lemonade. Look, I have some ice.

With that, he boldly opened the plastic that served as a curtain and introduced an arm to show him the ice.

-In case you're interested, you're invited to my house. I'll expect you, old man.

-The same Otón from the Ministry of Education? The same Otón, the guerrilla fighter? The same Otón who sent his guests to puke and shit at the door? The Otón who sends his cocks to destroy my roses?

-One and the same?... At your service.

-And now, you're screwing my wife?

-It's actually a social service. I'd like to consider myself an angel who consoles ill-married women... And just in case you'd like some lemonade, pass by my house... *Ciao*, I'm taking off.

Neto was overcome several times by rage and by finding himself with his archenemy again. "Wherever that man shows up –Shit! Soon, he had the feeling that someone else, someone from some Latin American had uttered that sentence.

-So, it was Oto, Otito, Ceroto... Why didn't it occur to me that it was that hack writer, if he lives right nextdoor. And I was looking for literary types at the office. And since I figured him to be my enemy, that he'd be my wife's as well. What an asshole I was . . . Hecky darn!

-Well, you didn't realize that the enemy of my enemy turned out to be my most delicious friend.

I finally found out, that poet bastard, that notorious motherfucker.

His head filled up with curses and he dwelled on so many things that he didn't realize what he was wiping with. Suddenly, he fell to the ground and couldn't stop pronouncing every time he scraped his beshitted backside:

-Forgive me, Mister President... I'm sorry,

Mister President... I won't do it again, Mister President... Liberty is written in blood, Mister President.

The last time he wiped his wet, hairy and disgusting old man asshole, he couldn't resist the temptation of seeing whom he had smeared. It was then when he discovered the face of the outgoing president. An image full of shit. And swollen with emotion, he said:

-Forgive me, Mister President. You don't deserve this, Mister President. It's no lie, but I'm sorry to see your face covered in shit. I think you should govern a better country like France, free Switzerland or industrial Belgium, but not here, full of shit. You would be the ideal man to guide the destiny of of the great people of Victor Hugo. Oh, I think I read that somewhere... Perhaps it's an expression of Victor Hugo. But I'm truly sorry, Mister President, one day I'll be your favorite.

Neto was sure this would happen, sooner or later. Before throwing the paper into the corner, he contemplated in detail the face of the outgoing president: an almost imperceptible smile outlined under a thick moustache of shit.

-I have the aura of an angel and I know I'm going to be the favorite among the favorites of his cabinet.

He exclaimed with pride when he left the pit latrine. It was cold. He found a black scarf on the clothesline and wrapped it around his neck. The wind brought him horrible ideas about how to avenge himself against Otón de la Vara. He decided to take a stroll through the outskirts of

Apopa. At every step, he imagined that he had the head of a literary man between his hands. He enjoyed it. His stiff tortilla face did not reflect the pleasant thoughts that every psychopath enjoys. He decided to destroy him, along with his cocks. "Vengeance is called fire and then . . ." he thought. He picked up his pace, with the black scarf covering half of his tortilla face. The pretender to favorite of the outgoing president was ugly and evil. As ugly and evil as Satan.

Susana Gusana

¡Ay Gusana, arro' con bacalao!
¡Habichuelitas tiernas, aguacate con hela'o!
¡Arro' con picadillo, yucaaaaaa!
¡Sal de la cueva! ¡Cua cua!

Son 13 & Mongo Santamaría.

The captain of the ship of fools was Susana Gu-
sana de la Giraldilla, a Gringa of treacherous
lineage, daughter of traitors to their native isle,
who had a serious face and soothing gestures.
Conceived in an alley behind the Giraldilla in
Old Havana, she was born in Miami after her
parents fled in search of their bank account.
They went to the USA to fuck things up there.
They searched for innertubes all over Havana
till they had enough to make a raft. They left the
Malecón at four in the morning, in front of the
Hotel Riviera, where her father had been a part-
ner of the famous gangster Meyer Lansky. They
carried enough water for a week, since Florida
is less than a hundred and fifty kilometers
away. But they didn't take into account the
currents, which carried them to the Bahamas.
On the eighth day, to conserve what water was
left, they decided to throw Granny into the sea.
Thanks to that practical act, they survived until
they were picked up by the US Navy. They were
so grateful for what they had done that they began to sing Inti Illimani's Guarapo y melcocha:

Si tomo guarapo por la madrugá

lo bueno se queda, lo malo se va.
Con esa melcocha tan bien amasá
Lo bueno se queda, lo malo se va.*

Just above the horizon, don Santiago, the old man of the sea, was fishing for a much desired swordfish. He had spent the last few months as unlucky as a blind man in a casino and this time, he was determined to end his bad luck streak. He had just finished spending ten hours under the blinding sun and he was almost ready to abandon his search again. At that moment, something bit on the hook. He was sure it was an enormous fish ready to fight to the death. Yes, it was truly enormous, but it wasn't a fish, but rather doña Bárbara Guarapo de Ochá, AKA "Granny." And she was ready to fight from beyond death because the boat had followed the whims of the cadaver out to sea. The old man's strength diminished at every turn. The "fish" continued drifting away without stopping as he slowly floated in the calm waters.

-If'n I lose sight of Havana's gleaming, it means we're going towards the east –he thought. I ain't never catched a fish so strong, not one that acted so strange. But, fuck it, whatta big fish! And shit fuck, they gonna pay bookoo bucks in the market if'n the meat's any good.

At that moment, the "fish" made a sudden jump against the boat. The old man fell against the prow and would've fallen into the water if he had not steeled himself and loosened up on the line. The old man stared constantly at the "fish"

---

* If I drink cane juice in the wee hours
the good stuff stays, the bad goes away.
With this taffy so well kneeded
the good stuff stays, the bad goes away.

to convince himself it was real. An hour passed before the first shark showed up. The old man sweated and wheezed. At every turn the "fish" peacefully and calmly made, the old man gained more line and he was sure that with two turns more, he'd have the chance to nail it with his harpoon.

-But now, I gots to reel it in, reel it in, reel it in, --he thought. I mustn't aim at the head. I gots to direct the blow directly to the heart. Be calm and be strong, fuck!

On the next turn, a wave threw the "fish's" back above the water, but it was still too far away, but with the growing waves, it peered more and more above the water, and the old man was sure that by reeling it in a bit more he could tie it to the boat.

He had prepared his harpoon and was ready to throw it. Now the "fish" grew near, looking smart but not a smart ass, but rather calm, without moving anything other than its big tail. The old man rowed with all his might to get closer. For an instant the "fish" folded over and drew near to the boat. But then, it straightened up and he began another turn.

–I done moved it –the old man said. This time I done moved it. With this little triumph, he felt up to snuff, ready to fuck a *quinceañera**, again he applied all the strength his old squalid body could muster to defeat the great "fish."

–I done moved it –he thought. Mebbe this time I can turn it. Throw hands –he thought. Hold tight, legs. Don't fail me brain. Don't fail me. You ain't never let me down. This time, I'm gonna turn it.

---

* Fifteen-year-old

He put all his effort into it, before the fish drifted away from the boat. He threw with all his strength. The "fish" partly turned over and then continued swimming, drifting away from the boat. He predicted the "fish" could kill him, but he was strongly determined to take it out of the water, and he didn't care if he had to pay with his life for trying.

–Fish –said the old man. Fuck, fish, you gonna die anyway. Do you gots to take me with you. Don't you leave me here alone like a worthless piece of shit.

-Fuck, this way I ain't gonna get nuthin –he thought. His mouth was too dry to speak, but now he couldn't reach the water.

-This time, I gots to reel it in –he thought. I ain't got many more turns in me. Yes, of course –he said to himself. He's ready for this and a whole lot more.

On the next go round, he was just about to beat it. But, once again, the "fish" straightened up and began slowly swimming away.

-Fuck, you're killin' me, fish —the old man thought. But you're right. Brother, I ain't never seen in my fuckin' life anything so big, so beautiful, more calm and more noble than you. Let's go, motherfucker... come and kill me. I don't give a fuck who kills whom.

-Now my mind is becoming confused –he thought. I gots to keep my head clear. Keep my head clear and learn to suffer like a man. Or like a fish –he thought.

-Clear up, head –he said in a barely audible voice. Clear up. Twice again the same thing has happened in the turns.

I dunno –the old man thought. Fuck, I dunno nuthin. But I'll try my luck again.

He tried again and felt himself give out when the "fish" turned. The "fish" straightened up and continued swimming like like he was the king of the sea, prouding shaking its tail in the air like Juan Gabriel in concert dancing the "Noa Noa."

For a moment, the old man thought he heard voices:

Cuando quieras tú, divertirte más.
Y bailar sin fin.
Yo sé de un lugar.
Que te llevaré (vamos al noa) y disfrutarás.
/(vamos al noa)
De una noche que nunca olvidarás.

¿Quieres bailar esta noche?
Vamos al Noa Noa Noa,
Noa, Noa, Noa, Noa, Noa
Noa, Noa, Noa vamos a bailar.

-Shit, fuck, could it be that fish is a buttfuck?... But I'll try again anyway –the old man declared, even though his hands had already turned to hamburger and he couldn't see well all the time.

He tried again and everything was just the same. "Fuck," he thought, and he felt himself falling again. "I'm gonna try again."

He wrapped all his pain into a ball and with what remained of his strength and pride, he faced the agony of the "fish." And it turned over on its back and smoothly swam on its side, almost touching the side of the boat with its beak: long, thick, silver with purple stripes and taking forever to die.

After a long hard battle till two in the morning, the "fish" finally gave in. The old man let the line fall to the floor and put his foot on it and lifted his harpoon as high as he could and launched it downwards with all his strength, he called upon the Apostol Saint James the Great -the Moor Slayer- and all the archangels, he threw it into the side of the "fish," behind its large pectoral fin, I mean right hand, which it held high in the air with an outstretched middle finger that once again invited him to commit an impure act. He felt the steel penetrate the "fish" and bent over it, penetrating it with the harpoon even more, and then he put all his weight into it.

Before he could cry victory, the "fish" came back to life, with death in its innards, and lifted itself from the water, showing all its great length and width and all its power and beauty. It floated in the air above the old man who was in the boat. Then it fell into the water with a splash that threw a jet of water over the old man and the whole boat. The old man felt his life slipping away. But he let go of the harpoon and let the line slip slowly through his bloody hands, and when he was able to see, he saw that the "fish" was on its back, belly up. The handle of the harpoon projected upwards at an angle like a flag and the Odyssean sea was stained with the blood red wine of its heart. First, it was dark as a sinkhole in the sea two kilometers deep. Then it straightened out like a cloud. The "fish" was silver on top of the tender waves.

The old man, crowned with happiness, no

longer believed that the "fish" was as enormous as before.

-It was so big, that it was like tying up a much bigger boat next to yours –he later said in the Bar La Terraza in the port of Cojímar.

All his strength would have been in vain if he could not take the "fish" to dry land. To his misfortune, a shark appeared. As as it approached on the port side where he had the "fish" tied on, the old man harpooned it in a single lethal blow. He escaped the fury of the shark, but the blood of the leviathan contaminated the sea with a vermillion trace that called out to its brothers to avenge themselves against the fisherman. The old man fought with them but they devoured half his prize. By early morning hordes of sharks had come, surely trained by Uncle Sam as part of his plot to overthrow the socialist economy of the First Free Territory of the Americas. At sun up there only remained the head, the backbone and the "tail," enough to testify to the greatness of his deed. He finally arrived in port. It was ten in the morning and the other fishermen had already set sail, so there was no one to help him take away the remains on the side of the boat. When he was finished, he went to take a siesta. In the afternoon, Manolito, his helper, anxious for news of his mentor, came to see how he was doing and gave him his word that he would go out with him. The other fishermen recognized Santiago's senility, when they saw the remains of the "fish," which was in no way a swordfish.

-Fuck, that old geezer is out of his damn mind. That's a woman's body!

And if Santiago had reached the woman before she expired, surely he would have married her. He had seen doña Bárbara Guarapo de Ochá many times when he was a sailor for the Havana Yacht Club and she went out with Hollywood stars such as Errol Flynn and drunken writers such as Ernest Hemingway. He always believed it was his destiny to join her and live off her fortune. In a certain manner his dreams came true.

-Don Santiago. Wait, that ain't no swordfish.

-You're right, kid. There's not enough left to give away at the market. But I'm gonna use it for fish bait. You'll see. This meat'll work better than a hundred kilos of sardines.

And so Santiago's dreams came true, because with the bait and Manolito's help, on his next time out, he caught a record swordfish that caught the attention of Fidel himself -may Eleguá protect him and Yemayá save him. *El Comandante* awarded him with the Order of Socialist Labor. With that, Santiago had something to talk about for the rest of his days.

The bigger the lie, more fools believe it. Who would believe that Susana Gusana, an American woman with an MBA from Harvard would work in the most dangerous country in the world; only a complete tard. Who would believe that she would go to El Salvador to earn a tenth of what she could earn in the USA? Only a full blown nutjob. But only ten per cent of a US salary was a rip off because that woman didn't have a fucking idea what she was doing. She lacked a degree in the section she was "directing." What teaching degree did she have? None! And so, when she thought about the quality of people around her, she didn't know and didn't want to know. But, as boss, she was legally responsible for all the crimes of the bandits who controlled her section. The poor idiot couldn't understand that she would be the first to to go to jail. The United States of America would not see with good eyes the embezzlement of funds by one of its citizens. They would send her to the slammer for the rest of her days. And the lunatics in the asylum, Neto, Juli Travi, Draculita and Morsa Amorfa gave thanks to Satan for that.

A Real Man

I've got to be a macho man,
macho, macho man.

Village People

Leonel Alfonso Menchaca Zúñiga dreamed about being the manliest of men, the man with the most hair on his chest, the most macho, the biggest cock on the block, the top motherfucker in all Central America. He was a macho from a long line of machos. He never saw his father help a woman in anything. Or better stated, fathers, because there was a long line of men he had to call "father." He noticed how each one, in turn, beat his mother, how they dumped her, one by one, and left her a whimpering mass thrown to the floor like a doormat. His life experience had taught him that women were something to fucked in every possible way.

If it weren't for more lucrative opportunities, he would have been completely happy and content where he dropped his umbilicus, Ciudad Delgado, better known as *Ciudad Delguaro**, since he never felt happier than when he was with his buds in the bars chasing women. It didn't matter that a woman who goes to bars in a slum is either a hag or a tard by nature. The only thing that mattered was to fuck a woman, especially if she was the squeeze of a friend.

---

* Booze City

During the war, he was Neto's unconditional advisor, his personal pimp who found him hens of all sizes and colors. "How do you like'em," he asked, "Chesty, leggy, dark, light? If I can find one, I'll send you one form my coop. Neto never forgot that his silence saved his life on several occasions.

He lost track of Neto when he received a scholarship to the Universidad de Valladolid. The scholarship came from the International Solidarity Fund of the Alianza Popular, now known as the Partido Popular, previously known as the Falange Española Tradicionalista y de las Juntas de Ofensiva Nacional Sindicalista. The Alianza, with funds from the Reagan regime, fervently sought to link up with other right wing parties –although reluctantly in the case of ARENA, but Washington was insistant and they had to comply.

Once in Spain, he began his Master's in Teaching Methodology. He completed his studies as slowly as possible since, in a very short time, he realized there were a large number of single women with elegant cars, mansions and immense amounts of money. Of course they were older, but with a good ironing every night, they looked younger. At the end of his first semester, he entered the service of doña Trinidad Carrero Alas de Alva, niece of the famous "Flying Admiral," don Luis Carrero Blanco. Leonel served doña Trini during the summer as a "pool boy" as she strutted around the swimming pool in a thong rubbing her body with creams and oils in a vain attempt to turn leather back into skin. During the spring, he helped doña Trini plant flowers in her vast garden. During the winter and fall, he accompanied her to the mountains, where he gave her massages after skiing, hunting or taking a walk through the woods. All year round, he was available for the woman's avid desires.

A little after receiving his degree, they found the body of doña Trini next to her shotgun. She hadn't even loaded a shell in the breech. Something had eaten her whole face –evidently a bear or a wild boar but there were traces of honey in her hair. Although there were claw or fang marks all over her body, around her neck the line was suspiciously straight. But the body had been in the woods for two or three weeks. Therefore, they couldn't concretely establish the cause of death. At home, everything was in order and her bank accounts were untouched. Years later, however, her daughter confessed that her illegal offshore accounts in the Cayman Islands were missing. But, since they only contained $5,000, it didn't seem a big deal. Her big illegal accounts were on the Isle of Man, Gibraltar, Jersey and Guyana.

Who would kill for so little money? Especially if the old woman had given him so much more for Christmas and birthdays? Perhaps it was his way of saying goodbye. He had already finished his degree and his visa was running out. The Socialists of the PSOE were in power and they weren't disposed to give a visa extention to any fascist, no matter how unimportant he was. The poet and philosopher Roque Dalton had already postulated: *No olvides nunca que los menos fascistas de entre los fascistas también son fascistas.*[*] There is no such thing as an enemy too small.

One can only imagine the shock, or rather rage, when Leonel Alfonso Menchaca Zúñiga opened the box at the main office of Sir Henry Morgan BankTrustCorp LLC in George Town, Grand Cayman and only found five thousand United States dollars. In his confusion, he had failed to realize that the account for $5,000,000 was at the branch in Georgetown, Guyana. The account numbers were the same, as were the names of the towns, but he didn't realize they were in very different countries. Since he had more or less spent the five thousand dollars on his trip and on luxury accomodations in the Cayman Islands, he lacked the resources to visit the fifty or so Georgetowns and George Towns scattered across the planet. That water was not for him to drink.

Leonel returned to El Salvador as impecunious as he had left. This was probably a good thing, since they would have killed him for ten bucks. He made a call to Neto and he found him a job at ESTAFASA as director of the coastal sector. Besides directing visits to schools in the coastal departments, he advised Neto whom to hire, whom not to hire. Evilhearts had a certain odor to them that only they can detect and Leonel was a bloodhound of evil. He could detect the sulfur in the soul of a miscreant as soon

* Never forget that the least fascist among the fascists are still fascists

as he entered the building. And as sure as lard asses hate skinny folks, the ugly detest the goodlooking and boneheads abhor the bright, evildoers are disturbed by the presence of the good. It's a Saussurian relationship inverse to the other, however, the skinny are skinny because they're not lard asses, the beautiful are defined because they're not ugly and the intelligent stand out because they're not idiots, but these are relationships in which the positive quality is nourished by the negative. The evil are parasites of the good and need them, therefore, just as a mosquito needs an artery, like a raptor needs prey. Evil perishes quickly in the absence of good. It was Leonel's task, therefore, to decide the level of goodness permitted in the organization. The good, besides, were necessary to disguise the secret missions that ESTAFASA carried out from time to time for its political mentors and the agents of the Great Colossus of the Frozen North.

Leonel, therefore, always carried out more or less legitimate work, since he tended to work in departments that were already under the thumb of ARENA. He only hired professional and presentable people who would give a good impression. Or well, let's say as professional and presentable as possible for someone from ARENA. There was no gang of monsters, thugs and freaks that worked with Neto. Leonel always insisted that he protect his gang by insulating them inside a group of innocents.

Neto's problem was that he didn't know or couldn't control himself. If someone did something in accordance with the official manual, he felt a tremendous urge to throw him out in the street. He couldn't sleep knowing that there was an able person in his office. His pecker didn't get hard when he realized there was a good and useful person in his section. He could only enjoy a good lay after firing a good employee. A good dominatrix, perhaps, could have sorted out his problems with the help of chains, handcuffs, whips and cattle prods. Only Susana Gusana's stupidity hid upper management from the fact that his section was a revolving door.

Leonel's great fault was that he couldn't realize how different he was from most of his employees. They were good, well most of them at least. There were a few like la Loyda who was hired for family reasons but most were scared of him. It was said that Interpol was looking for him for what he did in Spain, that he trafficked children and women during the war for military officers and civilian authorities who sold them to brothels and pornographers. They say he sold some blonde Chalatecas to the Taiwanese, Koreans and Arabs. They say Radha almost fainted when she saw him with Neto. In the midst of so much uncertain information, the only thing certain was his evil nature.

With the crew he had, it was difficult to find a woman to strike up an affair with. Women were becoming ever more indocile. Most were single mothers who fully understood from experience the etymology of the word "Son of a bitch."

*The Sand Castle Goes Out With the Tide
*

Acabou samba, a trabalhar:
Era o sol quando o samba acabou
De noite não houve lua, ninguém cantou

Noel Rosa.

One day, however, the party was over. With the imminent arrival of a new government from the opposition party, Doctor Arquímedes San Goyo was named to the directorate of ESTAFASA. Very different from his father, a lawyer who stole farms from illiterates, his greatest claim to fame was his clean hands. He was an apolitical technocrat, an ex-minister of the Ministry of Education, one of the few bureaucrats accepted by both sides. When he saw that Neto Tecolote was head of a department critically important to the Organización, he almost had a heart attack. He had read the report prepared by Rebeca Iwè Bard Godoy in great detail. He invited Neto to his office to inform him of the new protocol.

-This is an organization that receives money from foreign government and NGOs to implement progressive educational policies. Do you understand me, dumb ass?

-Yes, boss.

-I don't want you and your band of thieves putting everything in your pockets nor do I want any political proselytism in the public schools. Do you understand me, you imbecile?

-Yes, boss.

-The last thing I want is an assfuck coward

like you ruining everything by putting employees at one anothers' throats. Understand, idiot?

-Yes, boss.

-Get ready to find employment because you don't produce anything but problems. I'm giving you sixty days to find another position. I don't want bums, asslickers, rip offs, rapists and trouble-makers like you.

-Yes, boss.

-I'm gonna clean this outhouse because it smells like pure shit. And a turd is what you are, motherfucker.

-Yes, boss.

-And turds get thrown in the shitter and flushed.

-You're right, boss.

Neto left, thinking he had gone through the worst moment of his life. As an added charge, however, as soon as he got home, he received a call from a policeman, a certain friend of his, telling him that the triplets had been arrested in a "toxic storm." According to his friend:

-It was a Pricemart of drugs... they had ecstacy, weed, crank, crack, acid, and I don't know whatelse... But don't you worry... My buds and I are gonna take care of them... We're gonna teach'em good manners... show'em the right path... show'em what a group of real machos can do... When they get out Monday... they'll be good girls for the rest of their days... They won't even dare jaywalk.

Neto, when he heard that, drove to his friend's house pedal to the metal and, in the only act of valor and charity he would make in his whole life, he threw a wad of bills on the table and grabbed the girls without saying absolutely anything. All three were naked, screaming, bleeding, covered with the bodily fluids of a whole police station. There were Poloroid photos of them stuck to all the walls.

Neto checked out the details and discovered that the strongest drug at the birthday party was corn flour. It was a simple little birthday party with girls who had just given up their dolls. And they grabbed them in front of the house, as they were waiting for the taxi that was going to take them home. The police didn't even go into the house. The triplets said that Ricardo "Shit Hair" Guatón Basovia, a certain best friend of his, was waiting for them at the policeman's house and insisted that he be the first with each of them, and that he sent a message:

-Tell your Pop that this how you feel everyday when you're second banana to a ball-busting motherfucker.

Neto returned to his office and began calling all the asses he had kissed during his long career of ass licking. Finally, Silverio "El Tiburón" Sánchez, a nephew of General Sánchez Hernández remembered him. He was a captain when Neto arrived at Military HQ with a list of guerrilla sympathizers. He gave him an appointment for the following Monday.

*Aventures in Cockfighting *

Neto tried to keep a calm demeanor but he was about to burst out in rage. He hid with his door locked all day. When he got home, he had to do something to assuage his anger. He hadn't made love to his wife for years. Every since his daughter's pregnancy, Radha refused to let him near the triplets, not even to be in the same room as them. And with what had just happened, don't even think about it. To add to this, he realized how lonely he was with every woman who moved his wang.

La Chabelquis, to keep her job at ESTAFA-SA, had shown a certain flair for developing her linguistic competencies with Neto's wrinkled, atrophied ding-a-ling, but she didn't please him completely, because she was a Christian woman in her heart and would not consent to anyone deflowering her before matrimony.

Juli Travi had been his crony since they worked together in the Ministry of Education. He had never known a more perfidious viper than her, a friend with such professional abilities to turn cat into hare and back again. It was like being with a slut and a manwhore at the same time. Juli Travi, man and woman in one, he thought and yet, he was flooded with the terrible fear of losing his job. The day he least expected could knock him over and devour him completely. Who knows?... Maybe her thing-a-ling was bigger than his. In spite of that, he should've thanked her for acquiring half-dead chickens, so he could eat them raw in the bathrooms of ESTAFASA. After sex, this was his second favorite pleasure. Juli Travi was the only one who knew that secret.

What about la Morsa Amorfa? Better a date with Rosie Palm, Manuela's twin sister, that is, the affectionate Palm sisters who have consoled frustrated, abandoned, cuckolded lonely men since time began. Even if she were the last woman at ESTAFASA, he wouldn't even cover her face with the Panamanian flag, for fear of drowing in the canal.

Doña Merchita, for her part, had him up to here with her traditional boxing dance. She was a woman full of resentment ever since he began going out with la Chabelquis. Since those days, he ran her into the same corners as ever, but Doña Merchita neither went up nor down.

-Chickens!- Neto exclaimed. I must get me a hen ASAP. Only my niece is left but that poor thing is ugly, and besides, she got herself pregnant by that little drunk looking Arab. I can't fire him because he's protected by the Party and best friend of that gossip Ricardo. Besides, la Piluris could do me the favor, but she always has the sick obsession of getting knocked up by married men. And, even worse, I'm tired of her same old song and dance.

-Don Netooooh, you know why I love my husband sooooo much? Because I was pregnant by someone else, a married man, who was rather elderly and worked on the project, and since he didn't pay any attention to me, then my Luis Miguel married meeeeee...

-And that Luis Miguel had nothing to do with the famous Mexican star. He's got... ¡Ay!, but la Pirulis has gone too far by bad mouthing her husband's ugliness and ineptitude. Poor guy. It hurts me to say it: there are men who are assholes and others who are real assholes. He drives her around at 3, at 4, or any old time his mare demands it. He babysits for her. He takes care of kids that aren't his all day long. And on top of everything, she's going around looking for information for a divorce. Ha, ha, ha... The funniest thing is that he don't know nuthin. With that face of still water... Shoot. That's what's really screwed up about all this. You should be afraid of still water. It's best not to jump into five fathoms. And for all this, I ask what kind of dumbfuck I am. What a mess. The hens no longer sing in my coop.

Neto suffered from a terrible existential problem: Women no longer paid any attention to him. The last ones he hired were so liberal and had such a sense of self-sufficiency that they didn't even care if they were fired. Anything but sleep with a decrepit, worn out, disgusting man such as the aged Tecolote.

In the midst of his disgrace, the last thing he could put up with was to wake up to Radha's new and strange cock-like mania. He wasn't quite sure when it began. Bright and early one morning, at home he noticed her dancing down the hall, flapping her wings like a dying bird, dramatically bending her legs, crowing a sharp and annoying "cock-a-doodle-doo, cock-a-doodle-doo..." Just like crazy chickens crow. From time to time, she stuck her head out the window, and there, for a long while, contemplated the coop that belonged to that womanizing poet Otón de la Vara. In the coop, he raised 99 cocks and 20 hens. Some of the cocks were fighters. And according what to the triplets said, he was going to make the coop bigger to receive a hundred more cocks, a cordial gift from the association for solidarity of poets of Chile and Guatemala. Neto well understood the origin of Radha's cock-like attack. But bitter experience and many years of mis-marriage had taught him not to butt in to his wife's excentricities.

All these frustrations increased Neto's wrath. Perhaps that was the only authentic sentiment that his psychopathic unconscious permitted him to harbor. Otón de la Vara himself, avid reader of Boom literature novels, had called the rancorous old man a "living rancor" to his face.

-Hey, take it easy, man. Unstress yourself, man. Remember that in the war, first they killed those who were afraid, then they killed living rancors such as you. Lighten up with that lemonade I made you, man.

Neto was just about to throw the pitcher of cold lemonade at that attractive, puckish, jovial and eternally smiling face that would make anyone fall out of his stirrups. But he kept it in. He put some pieces of ice in his mouth to calm down. His scorpion nature permitted him to keep everything inside, in order to attack at the right moment. He promised himself:

-Just like that cold and condensed refreshment, I'm going to plan my revenge.

The first thing he did that morning was to enter the coop, just as the lazy poet was taking a siesta. He was just about to torture some cocks. What an urge he had to wring their necks, puck them and plant his teeth until the first flow of blood appeared. He felt such pleasure and urges to suck them! The scared face of that poor bastard!... As a strolling Tecolote, he went around and around the coop until his tecolotic instincts became still and put his mind to something else, he decided to scrutinize the books he always left on the patio table.

-What does that motherfucker read so much? What chapter is he reading with my wife?

The mixture of rage and impotence set fire to Neto's brain. For a while, he went around in a circle, clucking like a broody hen. He began to talk to himself. The talk became an argument. The argument became a fight until he started hitting himself and rolling on the ground. Finally, he got up and screamed: *Eureeeeeeeeeka!*

Neto was lost in his tecolotic thoughts until well after midnight. Finally, he decided to take out his shotgun and go cock hunting. He climbed up on the roof of his garage, almost directly above Otón's patio. He lied down on his belly and began firing until he killed the ninety nine remaining cocks. He left the hens to kill and eat later.

The next morning, a moving van arrived at Otón's house and a team emptied it out in less than an hour. Otón was convinced that he was dealing with a true psychopath and he took off to protect his family. Otón, who had suffered a year of torture in jail; who fought against the army in Chalatenango, who led a company of guerrilla fighers more than ten kilometers through the sewers from Cuscatancingo to the Zona Rosa, who organized platoons to execute traitors after any defeat, setback or error, gave in when faced with this madness. Only his laundry man knew for sure how scared he was.

All night long, Neto dedicated himself to making more ice shotgun shells. He put in new loads and powder, resealed the powder and added crushed ice. Just before dawn, he walked through the neighborhood and killed every cock he saw. See a cock, kill a cock. El Tecolote lives.

The next morning they found holes in all the *Pollo Campero* and *KFC* signs in Escalón and along the Bulevar de los Héroes. *El Diablo de Hoy* blamed Marxists students at the National University and the Jesuit UCA but they were all suffering tremendous hangovers when reporters arrived to interview them. The *Diario Co-Latino* acidly responded that those students were in no condition to carry any revolutionary act and that the real problem with the country was the lack of revolutionary spirit: "Be like Che!"

In his haste, Otón left behind twenty hens. Neto jumped over the wall and began to eat them raw –feet, feathers, bones, heads and all. One by one he ate them, leaving a trail of blood all over Otón's patio. He took off his clothes, painted his body from head to toe with chicken blood and exclaimed:

Kálo 'smi loka-kSaya-kit *

After finishing his words, he sat down for a long spell. A couple of hours later, he began to howl with pain. With his gizzard full of raw chicken, Neto ate gravel to quell the agony that the beaks and bones caused. Then, he began to cough, softly at first, but little by little cranking up as loud as a jet engine, until all the feathers came out. The wind carried them all over Apopa. He sat down again. There he remained the rest of the week.

---

* I am death, destroyer of worlds.

Extroitus

Llevá la luz ahora
Llevá la luz ahora
Que nos recuerda que el
Salvador anda ante nosotros
Que el Salvador es la luz
que alumbra el mundo.

Extroitus

And you shall see what are the wages of sin. I hope you've laughed as much reading this book as I did writing it. Only the last chapter and the appendices are left. Amidst your laughter, think well if Neto has received what he deserves or not. But don't forget to laugh as hard as you can. Enjoy your opportunity to be judge, jury and executioner all at once.

After finishing the book, talk to your buds. Tell'em how much you liked the book, but not right away. A minute after putting the book down, go to your squeeze, give that person some delicious kisses, start touching already until both of you end up in a seething, moaning mass. It's the least you can do after abandoning the love of your life for mere words. Then, pass that person the book and get ready for a few days of solitude.

This is a book meant to be read, so don't leave it on a bookshelf gathering dust and mold. Make the whole family read it and when they've all read it a dozen times, give it to someone who wants to read it. Don't worry about my royalties. I'll make more in a month at work than I'll make off this book in a lifetime. Happiness is a more important thing and if you can delight someone with an old copy of this book, then God will reward you in heaven. But if you have to sell it to buy diapers, He'll also remember you.

Before sending you on to read the last chapter, I want to thank you for reading my book. In the countries of Central America, there's never enough time to do what you want. That's why I appreciate you, dear reader.

The Revenge of the Cocks

At last, Monday arrived. Neto got dressed in his best gray suit. He put on some Old Spice and took off. He drove to the Ministry of Education. It had been years since he had seen it and the changes were notable. He went in and, awaiting him, was Silverio "El Tiburón" Sánchez, the nephew of the former president and guardian of his memory.

-Neto, how are you? So many years have gone by.

-That's right.

-But we never forgot the service you did for us during the war. I'm not going to be in the meeting but the Minister himself is going to take you to meet Mr. Big before he turns power over to the reds.

-Mr. Big?... Seriously?... No shit!

-Seriously, I told him about you and he wants to meet you.

The minister, Tránsito M. Morales, took him to San Jacinto in his new Mercedes to an enormous mansion. It seemed familiar. For a moment he thought about the General's presidential mansion but he couldn't be sure, since it was under reconstruction.

He entered an enormous salon with pink walls and reproductions of Greek nude athletic statues. There, waiting for him, was a man dressed in a purple robe, with a glass of cognac in his hand. Don Tránsito presented him to His

Excellency.

-Excellency, as Marx said, "This man, here at my side, looks and acts like a corrupt idiot... but don't be fooled... He is a corrupt idiot!"

-Marx said that?

-Groucho Marx said it.

-Neto! They've told me so much about you... A drink?

-Yes, Your Excellency, thank you very much.

-Tránsito, make him a special.

-But you look so different in person... You're really...

-Big... it's the makeup they put on me for the cameras. They also put on corrector for the bags under my eyes. A first-class make-up woman does my brow. That's why they call me the "Brow." You remember that song?

Affected by a musical energy that would have interested Freud himself, both men began to dance, opening their arms and joining their knees to produce a pronounced movement of the hips. That's how the great ones dance, the experts, the most talented dancers.

- And how did that go...?

-I'm the Brow. I'm the Brow. I'm the Brow... It's pleasure to be with Mr. Big.

-For me, it was a pleasure to dance with you... I mean, besides them putting more than enough makeup on me, to cover some facial imperfections, making me look natural and beautiful. Like those women in commercials saying: "What a great change, huh?"... Here comes your drink.

Neto accepted the glass Tránsito prepared for him and downed it all at once, like he had done so many years ago. He always believe that first act of valor was the beginning of his good luck streak, the rite of passage that made him a man. All of a sudden, everything went a bit fuzzy. He had trouble walking. Someone put on music, a very well known song but the lyrics seemed a bit strange:

*El cumba-cumba-cumba-cumbanchero chero chero
cumbanchero, cumbanchero que se va
el bongo-bongo-bongo-bongosero sero sero sero
bongosero, bongosero que se va
el tecu-tecu-tecu-teculero lero lero
teculero, culero que se va...*

Needing to take a leak, he stumbled to the bathroom. With a hand on the wall, he had problems pointing his thing-a-ling until a helping hand guided it towards the urinal. He then heard Mr. Big's voice:

-Let me help you. It looks like you're enjoying yourself too much.

While the host was aiming him, two muscular men pulled down his pants. They cuffed him and put him face down on a jaguar rug. Mr. Big yelled out:

-More music, buds. We're here to party. This ain't no morgue.

This time he heard the chorus that for so many years he had only heard in his nightmares. In the corner of his eye, he saw his wife and the triplets dancing naked to the beat, along with all his accumulated enemies who were still alive. Masses of people entered until the great hall was filled.

Tecolote, zopilote
hijo de cerote.
Neto Homero, Teculero,
te vamos a romper el trasero.

One by one, all his partners, buddies, cronies, lovers and enemies arrived to greet him with a poem or a song. Ricardo "Shit Hair" Guatón Basovia, his old friend from childhood, was the first to render homage by reading José Rosa Moreno's *El gato y el perro*:

Puss in Boots, gluttonous cat
Who was in every land a famous thief
Went into the pantry every day
By a hidden path,
And there with happiness
Got into the cheese, the bread and the bacon.
The owner saw the damage,
And couldn't guess who was the thief;
But once Puss in Boots whipped out
A large cake of bread,
Milord, the watchman,
His favorite dog,
Discovered the cat's able misdeed,
And taking it away from arrogantly:
-Traitorous, infamous cat,
it enrages me to see you!
He told him with in angry fit.
For evil and for thieving and for be ungrateful
Death will be your reward,
For robbery is punished with death!
How do you have, infamous one, the boldness
To stain our sacred code
That society has sanctioned?. . .
Oh, so much corruption here today!
Your life will be so short. . .
I will enjoy your agony so much. . .
And so much you said
You ate the cake so delicately.
In the world there is no shortage

Of worthy men
Who in morality and laws of lessons . . .
When the case arrives
Belie morality with their actions.

After his reading, he passed by Neto and whipped him with a bull prick lying on the table. He said farewell with the words: "you ain't worth dick to me, motherfucker."

Doctor Arquímedes San Goyo got up gently and slowly walked with his cane toward the center of attraction. Midway, he stopped before Rebeca Iwè Bard Godoy to kiss her hand. Then he continued walking, pausing every three or four step to catch his breath. Finally, he stopped in front of Neto and spoke with a voice still young and manly after so many years:

-For the good of the Fatherland, those who have violated her must be cast into a lake of fire -*Néstor delendus est!* This is the Law of the People, this is the Law of God –*Lex populi, lex Dei!* Those who have cut short the lives of so many promising individuals must pass through the purifying flames –*Vae victis!* Those who have lowered the sanctity of women must suffer eternal fire –*Mater tua in inferno mentulas fellat!*

Before returning to his chair, he lifted up his cane and began to rain down a thrashing, screaming "*accipe hoc!*" with every blow delivered untl he was exhausted. The assistants of Mr. Big had to carry him back to his seat. Before taking his seat, he exclaimed: "*Ab uno disce omnes.*"

The next to draw near was Rebeca. She approached Neto more stealthily than a doe. She kneeled to pray, asking mercy for us the living, so that we would not fall into temptation, that we have the wisdom to distinguish between opportunity and theft, between love and violation, between competition and hatred. After finishing her prayer, she stood up and asked the following questions:

-Neto, where would you be now if you had not chosen the path of the Adversary? Neto, what induced you to work toward the destruction of your family, your homeland and your world? Neto, how could you not have understood that since the moment you signed the black book of perdition, that you were a slave? Neto, how could you not have discovered that the only freedom is that of being a human being, of following your own true nature, of making yourself a disciple of goodness? Neto, with how many men of your power, your intelligence and astuteness, how much could all of you have won for the forces of Good?

While Rebeca returned to her seat, there stealthily approached the emissary of the Embassy, doctor Malcolm Shithead, to bid goodbye to Neto. He kneeled and began to slowly pronounce some fetid, tecolotic and unrecognizable words:

Nema. Olam a son arebil des, menoitatnet ni sacudni son en te. Sirtson subirotibed sumittimid son te tucis artson atibed sibon ettimid te, eidie sibon ad munaiditouq murtson menap. Attera ni te oleac ni tucis, aut satnulov taif. Muut munger tianevda. Muut nemon rutecificnas, sileac ni se iuq retson retap.

He whipped out a Q-Tip from a sealed bag, put the Q-Tip in Neto's mouth and swabbed the inside of his cheek. He left as stealthily as he arrived, only leaving behind a light trace of bile.

Finally, it was the turn of the Dignas and the Mélidas, women who had fought so many years against all the abuses that Neto perpetrated: against sexism, against sexual abuse, against rape, against the trafficking of women and children, against sexual harassment, against barriers set up against women in every sector of society. The Grand Digna and the Grand Mélida, in turn, pulled out a carpet knife to rip off his balls, which they held high to the applause of everyone. Later, they would put them, as a trophy in block of acrylic, next to John Wayne Bobbitt's penis. They took the occasion to make a brief speech.

-Friends, Brothers and Sisters: Today is a new day for El Salvador. I swear to you that this is the first day in this country that a woman has taken the most minimal measure of justice against the crimes of evil-doing men. It is incumbent upon us, the Salvadorans to labor to eliminate sexism in all its manifestations, so that the children of El Salvador may live in a country without artificial barriers. In the name of our beloved Mélida and so many other women whose lives were cut much too short, we take this meager measure of justice. We, Mr. Big, wish to express our profound appreciation for ending your mandate with an act of truth and appreciation without forgiveness nor forgetting.

At last... a government with human sense!

Now Draculita Chabelquis took her place beside the only man she'd ever loved. She put her face between Neto's legs, opened her mouth and bit his pirouline, ripping it off with all her might. Since she had spent so much time with Neto's pee-wee in her mouth, from now on she would never miss it.

-Neto, my Netito, your sweet pirouline is mine, it's mine forever.

Upon witnessing such a spectacle, la Morsa Bisontina Amorfa ran straight to Neto to confess her love. She caressed his hair.

-Neto, I could never tell you how much I adored you, how much I adore you. I could write the saddest verses tonight. I loved you and always wanted you. Wherever you go after your brief residence on earth, wherever you go walking, whenever you're walking around, do not forget that I, la Morsúbela, was the only one, the real one who loved you.

Before leaving Neto, she gave him a long kiss that seemed to last minutes, if not hours. She explored the deepest part possible of his alimentary canal with her tongue, beyond the gullet to his gizzard. She had just finished when Neto responded with a tremendous bout of vomiting. He puked a week's worth of food –bones, claws and chicken beaks flew through the air.

In that moment they called Otón de la Vara. Otón, always a gentleman, approached slowly and quietly with a cock under each arm.

-Assfuck Teculero, remember me? I swore I would get revenge and here I am ready to rip your eyes out. You escaped justice so many times, but not today. Today there is no escape. Even your masters have abandoned you, your masters who lifted you up, have now let you down. Look, Assfuck Teculero, look, what I bring you, a pair of cocks, two of the cocks you tried to eradicate from the earth. Here they are, here to claim vengeance from you.

That said, Otón placed them on Neto's eyes to blind him but they just stayed there, still and Neto was completely quiet until one of the two shat in his right eye and Neto began to howl. Very little, but still justice, and Otón slowly and quietly left with his eternal smile.

After Otón, Susana Gusana approached Neto. With her squealing, tacky, high-pitched voice, she began to speak.

-Ay, Netito!... I had so much to tell you but something more important happened. I couldn't decide what color blouse to wear, pink or white. Anyway, I wish you happiness in the Great Beyond.

The last to render homage was his wife, Radomira Bojórquez, accompanied by the triplets and her grandson. Esperanza, the child's mother, held her son high and shouted to him:

-Look, you little bastard, look well... they're gonna burn your father alive.

Upon hearing those words, his face of stoic stupidity turned into one of intense terror. He let out all the accumulated screams over so many years –66 years of horror, of a wasted life.

At Neto's side, Mr. Big struck up a conversation with the Adversary, who wore, beside his habitual black suit, a face of disappointment.

-My big Mr. Big, what happened?... What did we do wrong? In spite of all my efforts we only only lasted twenty damn years. We were so close to reaching my dream of turning the country into the first branch of Hell in the world of the living. And you took away my most loyal servant.

-I'm sorry, Eminence, it had to be done. The reds won and we had to sacrifice a few choice individuals. If we didn't, that band of utopian idiots would have started a series of investigations and we'd all be in Zacatraz. So, for offering them the heads of a few dumbasses, they'll even praise us for leaving them a clean government. It so turns out that a few delusioned individuals, stirred up by the country's name, seem to believe that country belongs to Jesus Christ, when it has always belonged to men of genius and steel, those of us who have the wherewithal to defend our rights.

-Agreed, this country is mine! Only the name belongs to my Enemy. And I could use loyal and servile servants to complete the first step in the conquest of the world of the living.

-But look at what we have done: the highest rate of crime and homicide in the world; the total degradation of women –now turned into slaves, whores or punching bags; gangs of demons so cruelly successful that we export them to all of Central America, Mexico and even the USA; the privatization of almost the entire economy, with the exception of air, and we were on the verge of obtaining all this when we lost the elections; hypocritical mega-churches of thousands of tithes to further your mission; the largest money-laundering banking industry in the region; the largest airline in the world –all at your service, Eminence. The sacrifice of some of your agents is nothing compared to all this... And this macabre festival has given you the opportunity to see your worst enemies close up and study their weaknesses.

-You're right, Big Mr. Big, and imagine that I thought you were a dumbass all this time. You'll have a spectacular future with me. I don't know what I'd do in this country if it weren't for you and the Reverend.

-We've had some setbacks, Eminence, but in five years we'll be in power again, stronger than ever. We'll leave a few time bombs, such as pensions, the VAT tax, the banking sector, public transportation, electricity and water. It's all ready to blow up in their faces.

Neto, meanwhile, howled in agony. The stronger Neto screamed, the stronger the invitees sang until they all broke him. . . . With that, everyone applauded and began to sing the Cock Boys' Anthem:

Cock-a-doodle-deer, the cocks are all here
Cock-a-doodle-dive, for having survived
Cock-a-doodle-dud, by the love of their buds
Cock-a-doodle-duck, to claim revenge from this
assfuck.

As they finished the song, they soaked Neto in gasoline. Juli Travi, fulfilling her role of modeling before the ESTAFASA people, dressed in a leather miniskirt and red knee-length patent leather book, pulled out a lighter and in a few minutes, Neto was turned to ashes. A blast of wind passed through the house, carrying his remains aloft, mixing them with the ashes of the sugarcane harvest, scattering them all over the city like a great plague amongst the entire citizenry. Now Neto was free to serve his master in the underworld. Everyone screamed good cheer in unison. In the background, there was a flag with the motto of the CIA.

VERITAS LIBERABIT VOS
LA VERDAD OS LIBERARÁ
THE TRUTH WILL SET YOU FREE

Printed in the United States of America
by Casasola LLC

MMXV